Are You ~~Normal~~, Mr. Norman?

and Other Short Plays

by David Henry Wilson

A SAMUEL FRENCH ACTING EDITION

SAMUEL FRENCH

FOUNDED 1830

New York Hollywood London Toronto

SAMUELFRENCH.COM

TABLE OF CONTENTS

For Lisbeth

Are You Normal, Mr. Norman?

a play in one act

CHARACTERS

NORMAN
A MAN
ANGELA
MR. LUGG
ALICE
A POLICEMAN

SCENE: Dentist's waiting room and surgery
TIME: The present

ARE YOU NORMAL, MR. NORMAN? was first presented by Jimmy Wax at the Hampstead Theatre Club on February 27th 1966 with the following cast:

A MAN .... Frank Wilson
NORMAN .... Philip Bond
ANGELA .... Marika Mann
MR. LUGG .... Nigel Hawthorne
ALICE .... Cheryl Conte
POLICEMAN................................. Frank Taylor

Directed by Ian Watt-Smith
Stage Manager—Christine Roberts

Are You Normal, Mr. Norman?

SCENE: *The waiting room, on extreme left of stage. This is very small, containing a single chair, and a table with one magazine, in very bad condition. There is a door in the left-hand wall. For the time being, the rest of the stage is in darkness.*

NORMAN is sitting in the chair, leafing through the magazine. After a fairly long silence we hear a loud moan from the other side of the stage. NORMAN looks up in horror. Silence. Another moan, louder. Greater horror from NORMAN. The moan rises to a scream, followed by a MAN's voice shouting "Let me go! Let me go!"

NORMAN rushes to the door left, and tugs at it. The door will not open. The shouting continues, and NORMAN continues to tug in vain.

A MAN, holding his hand to his mouth, rushes on from the right-hand side of the stage. He goes straight past NORMAN moaning all the time, pulls open the door, goes out and slams the door behind him. NORMAN tugs at the door again, but it remains tightly closed.

NORMAN. (*rather desperately*) Oh, open up, open up! I want to get out of here!

(*ANGELA comes in from the right-hand side. She is wearing a white coat, but even this cannot disguise the fact that she is every man's dream.*)

ANGELA. Good morning. (*As soon as NORMAN sees her, he moves guiltily away from the door, grinning sheepishly.*) I do hope you weren't too put off by all that noise. He was a dreadful patient.

NORMAN. Oh no, not at all, I . . . not at all. (*Swallow*)

ANGELA. We're hoping to make the other room sound-proof soon, so that patients won't be distressed by all the noise.

NORMAN. Oh, yes, rather a good idea.

ANGELA. Anyway, don't worry. Mr. Lugg is very gentle.

7

NORMAN. Yes, yes, I'm sure he is. I . . . I have complete faith in him.

ANGELA. (*sitting down*) Now there are just one or two questions I have to ask you, so we'll give Mr. Lugg time to recover, shall we?

NORMAN. Er, questions?

ANGELA. Just a formality. What's your name, please?

NORMAN. Norman. (*She writes everything down.*)

ANGELA. Christian names?

NORMAN. Norman.

ANGELA. Oh. And your surname?

NORMAN. Norman. Norman Norman. Silly, isn't it?

ANGELA. Married or single?

NORMAN. Married.

ANGELA. Yes. Your age?

NORMAN. Twenty-seven.

ANGELA. Wife's age?

NORMAN. Twenty-four.

ANGELA. Twenty-four. Three years. That's quite all right. Children?

NORMAN. Yes, two. A boy and a girl.

ANGELA. Ages?

NORMAN. The boy's four and the girl's two.

ANGELA. And how old were you when you were married?

NORMAN. Twenty-four. . . . er . . . twenty-three. Well you see . . .

ANGELA. Yes, I see.

NORMAN. Look, I only want him to have a look at one of my teeth . . .

ANGELA. Exact address?

NORMAN. Pardon?

ANGELA. Your address?

NORMAN. 14, Crescent Road, Wandsworth.

ANGELA. Telephone?

NORMAN. (*increasingly mystified*) Wandworth 0864. But . . .

ANGELA. It's just a formality, Mr. Norman. For the records. I think we can go in now.

(*The lights go up on the right-hand section of the stage. This is the surgery. In the centre is a large, flat-surfaced board, with leather straps hanging down from it. A cupboard stands on the right, and there is a chair in front of it. Dan-*

gled over the back of the chair is a blood-stained cloth, and sitting in the chair is MR. LUGG. He is also wearing a white coat. His head is in his hands, until the moment when AN-GELA leads NORMAN in, and then he looks up. His manner is very friendly, and he rises to shake hands with NOR-MAN.)

ANGELA. Mr. Norman.

LUGG. I'm pleased to meet you, Mr. Norman. Very pleased to meet you. I hope you weren't too shaken by the unpleasant scene of a few moments ago.

NORMAN. Oh no, not at all.

LUGG. We do occasionally have difficult patients, and it's so trying on the nerves. I intend to have the surgery made sound-proof one of these days, to avoid all the distress.

NORMAN. Yes, your receptionist was . . .

LUGG. Of course that wouldn't help us very much, but it would stop patients from becoming upset. Now then, Mr. Norman, what's the trouble?

NORMAN. It's my back tooth, here—(*pointing to it, with mouth open*)—it's been sort of twingeing.

LUGG. Yes, yes, trouble with your teeth. Now there are just one or two questions I have to ask you before we begin. Just a formality. (*He sits down, and produces paper and a pen.*)

LUGG. Your name, please?

NORMAN. Oh your receptionist has already taken down all the details.

LUGG. Name?

NORMAN. Er . . . Norman.

LUGG. Christian names?

NORMAN. Norman. But your . . .

LUGG. Your name is Norman Norman?

NORMAN. Yes but . . .

LUGG. Is that right, Angela?

ANGELA. Norman Norman.

LUGG. I see. Are you married or single?

NORMAN. I'm married. Your receptionist already has this in-formation. (*He turns to her for help, but gets no reaction.*)

LUGG. Your age?

NORMAN. (*resigned*) Twenty-seven.

LUGG. Wife's age?

NORMAN. Twenty-three.

LUGG. Twenty-three.

ANGELA. Twenty-four. (*LUGG looks up very sharply.*)

NORMAN. Oh, I meant twenty-four. Sorry, I was confused . . .

LUGG. Don't worry, Mr. Norman, don't worry. Twenty-three or twenty-four?

NORMAN. Twenty-four. Silly of me . . .

LUGG. Twenty-four. Three years. Yes, that's good, that's a good sign. Any children?

NORMAN. Yes, I . . . a boy and a girl.

LUGG. Ages?

NORMAN. The boy's four and the girl's two.

LUGG. And your age when you were married?

NORMAN. (*again looking at ANGELA for help, and getting none*) Er . . . well I . . .

LUGG. Twenty-four?

NORMAN. Er . . . yes, just.

LUGG. Don't worry, Mr. Norman — it's all just a formality. Now your exact address?

NORMAN. 14, Crescent Road, Wandsworth.

LUGG. And your phone number?

NORMAN. Wandsworth 0864.

LUGG. Is that all correct, Angela?

ANGELA. All correct.

LUGG. Good. Just one little inconsistency, but . . . (*smiling*) . . . we can overlook that, can't we?

NORMAN. Yes. Thank you. I . . .

LUGG. Now there are one or two other little questions before we begin. Won't take a minute. Your mental history.

NORMAN. I beg your pardon?

LUGG. Mental history.

NORMAN. (*after slight pause*) I don't . . . quite understand.

LUGG. Would you say you were normal, mentally?

NORMAN. Oh I see. Yes, yes, I'm quite normal. I've never had any trouble.

LUGG. Good. And wife?

NORMAN. Yes. You'll never find a more ordinary, normal couple than Alice and me.

LUGG. Normal?

NORMAN. Yes. (*Pause*) Yes, normal.

LUGG. Is your marriage happy?

NORMAN. Absolutely, yes. We're very happy indeed. Look, I . . . I only wanted you to have a peep at . . .

LUGG. But you do have tooth-ache.

NORMAN. Yes! That's why I've come to you . . .

LUGG. Exactly, and very wise too, Mr. Norman. Very wise. Well we must see what we can do for you then, shall we?

NORMAN. Yes, I'd be very glad if . . .

LUGG. Sit down then.

NORMAN. Er . . . where's the . . . er . . . chair?

ANGELA. This way. (*She leads him to the board.*)

NORMAN. But this isn't a chair.

ANGELA. Just stand here please. (*He stands against the board, quite bewildered. ANGELA ties the straps, one round his ankles, one at waist height, pinning his arms to his sides, and another round his throat.*)

NORMAN. Look. . . . what. . . . what's this. . . .

ANGELA. It's all right, Mr. Norman, don't worry. (*Smiling at him*) I'll be here. (*LUGG has been busy looking into his cupboard. Eventually he brings out a hammer and chisel, and an all-purpose electric drill.*)

NORMAN. Oh my God!

ANGELA. Don't worry. (*LUGG takes off his white coat, and we see that he is wearing a very tight, superman-type black costume, and that he is extremely powerfully built.*)

LUGG. Angela. (*She takes the tools from him, and places them neatly at NORMAN's feet. He watches, rigid with horror.*) Now then. (*His manner has changed completely. Every movement and every word is indicative of enormous power, and it is a power in which he revels.*) Mr. Norman, you say you are suffering from tooth-ache. Why?

NORMAN. Why? I. . . . I am.

LUGG. What is the reason for this pain?

NORMAN. I. . . . I don't know. That's why I came. . . .

LUGG. It is an established fact, is it not, Mr. Norman, that pain must have a *cause*?

NORMAN. Yes. . . .

LUGG. What is the *cause* of your pain? (*Silence*) Well?

NORMAN. I don't know. I. . . . I don't know.

LUGG. Open your mouth. (*NORMAN opens his mouth.*) Torch. (*ANGELA goes to the cupboard, and brings LUGG a torch. LUGG remains quite a distance away from NORMAN.*) Open it wider! (*He directs the beam at NORMAN's mouth.*) Wider, Norman, wider! (*After scanning along the beam for a moment or two, he switches off.*) Close your mouth! There's nothing to be seen. What's the matter with you, Norman? (*NORMAN is now too miserable to speak. After pacing up and down:*) Now keep calm, Norman. Don't panic. We're here to help you. (*More pacing, then he stops, decisively.*) Mr. Norman, have you ever in your life had the feeling that you are alone, and that life is insecure, and that no-one can ever really understand you? Have you?

NORMAN. Yes, yes I have.

LUGG. A feeling that no matter what you do, no matter how many people you know or think you know, no matter how active and social you are, at the end there is nothing but yourself, in sad isolation. Have you ever had that feeling?

NORMAN. Yes. I have had it.

LUGG. And you think you're a normal person?

NORMAN. I am a normal person.

LUGG. Mr. Norman, I have never had that feeling. I have never felt anything other than complete unity with the universe. I have never felt isolated, or lonely, or insecure. But Mr. Norman, I am normal. Do you understand?

NORMAN. I. . . . I don't know. . . .

LUGG. I am normal. And yet you say you are normal! Angela, have you ever had such a feeling as Mr. Norman has described?

ANGELA. No, Mr. Lugg.

LUGG. No. So you see, Mr. Norman. You are not normal. We're coming to the truth, aren't we? Slowly but surely we're approaching the truth, but there's a lot more, a lot more, isn't there? A lot more. . . . abnormality hiding beneath the surface. It's no use pulling against the straps, Mr. Norman, they won't give way.

NORMAN. What are you trying to do to me?

LUGG. (*violently*) Help you! Help you, Norman! You came here for help, and now, by God, you will be helped! (*Calmer*) You say you have toothache. And because you have a pain, you come to me to put it right for you. Cause and effect — you have a pain, I must put it right. So simple for you. Norman, the world is full of pain. Millions of people are in pain. And millions of people are crying out for help that doesn't come — crying to you, not just to me, to you, Norman, you! And do you hear them? Do you?

NORMAN. Well I. . . .

LUGG. Millions! And you don't hear those voices! Angela, do you hear the voices?

ANGELA. Yes, Mr. Lugg.

LUGG. Yes. I hear them. Angela hears them. And you don't hear them. Are you normal, Mr. Norman? You see what I mean? There is something very wrong with you — this isolation, and this. . . . spiritual deafness. Are you happily married?

NORMAN. Yes, I told you. . . .

LUGG. Then perhaps there's some hope there. (*He sits down. ANGELA takes off her white coat. She is wearing only a slip, which reveals a good deal of what she has — and she has a good deal. She comes very close to NORMAN, who cannot take his eyes off her body. LUGG watches attentively. ANGELA, with a highly provocative smile on her face, rubs gently against NOR-MAN, who pulls against his bonds. She runs her fingers over his face. LUGG moves swiftly but quietly behind NORMAN, and loosens the strap that binds his arms. NORMAN at once embraces ANGELA, and tries to kiss her. ANGELA thrusts his arms down, and LUGG seizes them, and binds NORMAN again. ANGELA puts on her white coat.*) Just as I thought. Just as I thought. Disgusting!

NORMAN. What. . . .

LUGG. Norman, you're a married man!

NORMAN. I know, I. . . .

LUGG. You claim to be happily married, you have a wife and two children, and yet at the first opportunity you would betray your family.

NORMAN. I. . . . I wasn't betraying. . . .

LUGG. (*angrily*) Betraying! You wanted to kiss Angela, didn't you? Didn't you?

NORMAN. Well so would anybody!

LUGG. Anybody? Any married man?

NORMAN. She's very attractive.

LUGG. So you would kiss her, and betray your own wife.

NORMAN. (*weakly*) Well anybody would. (*LUGG nods to ANGELA, who takes off her coat again. This time she comes to LUGG, brushing up against him, running her fingers over his face, etc. He remains absolutely motionless.*)

LUGG. I think that's enough, Angela. (*She puts on her coat again.*) Mr. Norman, I am a normal person. I have a wife and four children, you understand. You say you are normal.

NORMAN. I am! I am!

LUGG. (*extremely overbearing*) Mr. Norman, are you, at this moment, happy?

NORMAN. No I'm not! I. . . .

LUGG. You would like to be released, and free to go, wouldn't you?

NORMAN. Yes I damn well would!

LUGG. And yet. . . . and yet, Mr. Norman, when I released your hands, you made no attempt to free yourself, did you? Would not a normal person have tried to untie that strap, and then that one, to get away, to recapture his liberty? Wouldn't he? (*NORMAN looks miserable.*) Instead you, a man who claims to be happily married, could do nothing but attempt to embrace a woman whom you have known for scarcely ten minutes. Are you normal, Mr. Norman?

NORMAN. It was wrong, I know, but. . . . she attracts me.

LUGG. So much for your marriage. This is a serious case, a very very serious case.

NORMAN. (*rather plaintively*) Please let me go!

LUGG. Go? Like this? Mr. Norman, you are in need of help. You're sick. A very sick man. Think of your wife — at every moment in danger of being married to an adulterer; your children living in a home that might soon be ruined through your inability to control your animal desires. This, and your innate selfishness and unawareness of the sufferings of other people make you into a menace to society, Mr. Norman. You are a monster of our age, and my horror is that there may be others like you.

NORMAN. Um, look, I really must go, my wife'll be expecting me. Perhaps I can. . . . come back. . . .

LUGG. Angela, kiss him. (*She goes to NORMAN, and gives him a long, very tender kiss, which he resists briefly, but returns with the minimum of persuasion. When the kiss is over, ANGELA steps back and NORMAN lets out a "Whew!" and licks his lips appreciatively.*) Mr. Norman, how is your tooth?

NORMAN. My tooth? Oh my tooth! It's fine. It doesn't hurt at all.

LUGG. (*intensely*) But I haven't touched your tooth, Mr. Norman, have I? No-one has touched it, you've had no treatment!

NORMAN. No, well, it was just a twinge, perhaps it's all right now. I. . . . I needn't trouble you any more.

LUGG. There was never anything wrong with your tooth! You have come here for some other reason, Mr. Norman — as I suspected, the *cause* lies deeper, much deeper. (*He sits down again.*) The problem is: how to make you into a presentable human being. (*He ponders deeply. NORMAN visibly summons up new forces.*)

NORMAN. Now look here, Lugg. I've had enough of this! You just untie these straps, and stop this business! You hear me? I've had enough of your game, and now I'm going home! Do you hear? Lugg, untie these damn straps! Angela, or whatever your name is, untie these things. (*He pulls hard and in vain.*) Lugg!

LUGG. (*standing up*) It may be necessary to do a full amputation. (*Slight pause*)

NORMAN. (*hushed*) What?

LUGG. Angela, pincers. (*ANGELA goes to the cupboard, and brings out a large pair of pincers, which she hands to LUGG. NORMAN screams. The noise shocks LUGG.*) Sh! Be quiet, man, we're trying to help you.

NORMAN. (*beginning to break up*) No please, what are you going to do? Don't do that, please!

LUGG. Put the other tools back, Angela, we shan't need them. (*She picks up the other tools, and replaces them in the cupboard.*)

NORMAN. Oh God, what are you going to do to me? What do you want from me? How much. . . . how much money do you want?

LUGG. Angela, what was Mr. Norman's phone number?

ANGELA. (*referring to notes*) Wandsworth 0864.

LUGG. I think perhaps I should phone Mrs. Norman first. You see, Mr. Norman, some people are very sensitive about these matters, and I have no wish to break up your marriage. If your wife will cease to love you, then an amputation is out of the question, but if she will still love you when you have had a complete amputation, then it might save your marriage. Do you see?

NORMAN. What are you going to do to me?

LUGG. The phone, Angela. (*ANGELA brings him the phone from the cupboard, and holds it for him.*) Is your wife sufficiently devoted to you, Mr. Norman, to have you back?

NORMAN. For God's sake let me go!

LUGG. Well, we shall soon see. (*He dials and waits.*) Hello? is that Mrs. Norman? Ah, good morning, Mrs. Norman, my name is Lugg. I'm a dentist, and your husband has paid me the honour of coming to me for help today. . . . yes he is. . . . Mrs. Norman, it may be necessary for me to extract all his teeth, I'm afraid, and I felt I must telephone you first to hear your reaction. . . . Yes, all of them, I'm afraid. . . . No, it's not possible at present. . . .

NORMAN. Alice, get the police! The police! Help! Help!

LUGG. Gag him! (*ANGELA immediately puts a gag over NORMAN's mouth.*) No, no, Mrs. Norman, nothing at all. . . .

he is just a little upset, naturally, but it's you he's worrying about
. . . he's afraid you may not love him any more when he has no
teeth, you see. . . . No, Mrs. Norman, it's impossible, the nurse
has just given him a sedative, and he's asleep . . . The question is
whether you will be prepared to have him back after the operation. . . . Yes, it is necessary, and I only wish it weren't. Good,
good, that will be a great comfort to him, Mrs. Norman, I knew
I could count on you. I am touched by your devotion. . . . Yes,
he'll be home soon. . . . Goodbye, Mrs. Norman. (*He hangs up,
and ANGELA takes the phone back to the cupboard.*) That
problem is settled. Your wife loves you truly, Mr. Norman, and
will continue to love you, even afterwards. Gag, Angela. (*She
removes the gag.*)

NORMAN. Please, please let me go! I'll do anything you want!

LUGG. Mr. Norman, you do understand, don't you, why I
have to do this?

NORMAN. Please!

LUGG. It is for your benefit. Angela, sterilize the pincers. (*He
gives them to her, and she breathes on them two or three times.*)
You will thank me one day, Mr. Norman. You see, normal is a
word we use so loosely, and so ignorantly.

NORMAN. I've understood, Mr. Lugg, I've understood! I'll
change my life from now on! You can let me go! I've understood!

LUGG. It won't take very long. Angela, the cloth. (*She places
the blood-stained cloth round NORMAN's neck. He struggles
violently to free himself.*)

NORMAN. Please! Please! Oh God!

LUGG. And at least you will have the consolation that you'll
never get tooth-ache again. Practice board, Angela. (*She goes to
the cupboard, and brings out a piece of wood, with several nails
embedded in it. She holds the wood in front of LUGG.*) You'll
be a different man after this, Mr. Norman. Wiser, more com-
passionate. Compassion is the secret. (*While he talks, he begins
to tug nails from the board, each one with a deliberate, studied
gesture.*) This loneliness of yours will disappear, this feeling of
isolation. And you'll lose these animal desires that are so dangerous for your peace of mind and, of course, for your marriage.

NORMAN. Mr. Lugg, there's no need for you to take my teeth
out! Believe me, I've understood. I promise to do anything you
want. . . .

LUGG. Yes, I think I'm ready now. (*He flexes his wrists.*)

NORMAN. Mr. Lugg, listen to me! Please! I've understood! I've been a fool, I've been blind, but now I understand.

LUGG. Mr. Norman, you cannot understand. No-one can understand. Only when a change has taken place, a permanent change, can there be understanding. Angela. (*She goes behind NORMAN, who once more struggles fiercely but in vain to get free. LUGG approaches him.*)

NORMAN. Get away from me! Get away! Help! Help! Help! (*As LUGG reaches him, he closes his mouth tightly.*)

LUGG. Open your mouth, Norman. (*NORMAN keeps his mouth tightly closed.*) Angela. (*She digs her fore-fingers into the sides of NORMAN's neck. With a loud "AH!" he opens his mouth. She keeps up the pressure. LUGG stands directly in front of NORMAN, and we see the first flourish, accompanied by a moan from NORMAN.*)

LUGG. Bowl. (*ANGELA goes to the cupboard, and fetches an enamel bowl.*) On the ground. (*She places it by his feet, and he drops the tooth into it, with a sharp 'ting'. ANGELA returns to her post behind NORMAN, who continues to moan.*) Now then, keep your mouth open, Norman. (*ANGELA exerts the pressure again, and at great speed, LUGG 'extracts' one tooth after another, dropping each one into the enamel bowl. NORMAN's moaning is continuous.*) There we are. Finished. Cloth. (*He sits down in his chair, evidently exhausted. ANGELA holds the cloth to NORMAN's mouth.*) Release him. (*ANGELA releases NORMAN. He himself holds the cloth up to his mouth and remains, knees buckling slightly, head bowed, and still moaning, up against the board. ANGELA takes the bowl to the cupboard. NORMAN sinks to his knees, still holding the cloth to his mouth. ANGELA remains by the cupboard. LUGG, breathing hard:*) My task is difficult. Age is beginning to tell on my strength. Time was when I could take on ten men, one after the other. Pincers. (*He holds them up, and ANGELA takes them from him, and puts them in the cupboard.*) Tell him he's free to go. (*ANGELA goes to NORMAN.*)

ANGELA. Mr. Lugg says you're free to go. (*NORMAN remains kneeling, with head bowed.*)

LUGG. Has he gone?

ANGELA. (*returning to LUGG*) He hasn't moved.

LUGG. White coat. (*She gives him his white coat.*) Help me. (*She helps him to put it on. His movements are very slow and painful.*) Now go to him. (*She goes to NORMAN, and kneels beside him, putting her arms round him, and holding him closely.*)

ANGELA. You'll be all right. Your wife still loves you, and the pain will soon pass. Don't cry, Mr. Norman. You're free now. Don't cry.

LUGG. Bring him here. (*She guides NORMAN over to LUGG, both of them still on their knees, NORMAN's head still bowed. LUGG does not look at NORMAN, but reaches out his hand until he has found NORMAN's head.*) My poor friend. My poor friend. This is the agony of the ages. This is the sorrow for which we have grieved since we were first created. I can't look at you. I feel for you. I feel your pain, and I feel your despair at things gone that can never be brought back. But this is normal. I can't look at you. But believe me, this is normal, and must be lived with. Help everybody, regardless of colour or creed. (*With great emphasis*) You are not the first. Remember that, my poor friend, you are not the first! Now go. (*Towards the end of this speech, NORMAN has slowly raised his head. Although the lower part of his face is still hidden by the gory cloth, his eyes betray the massive hatred that is building up in him, and these eyes become riveted on LUGG.*)

ANGELA. Mr. Norman. It's time to go.

LUGG. Go, Mr. Norman, to the wife who loves you. The animal has gone for ever, and in time the isolation will go too. You will be free.

ANGELA. Mr. Norman. (*With a snarl NORMAN leaps at LUGG, pressing the bloody cloth over LUGG's face, and lifting him bodily by his neck. There is no resistance from LUGG, as NORMAN hurls him against the board, snarling all the time, and fastens him there with the straps. ANGELA remains kneeling on the ground.*)

NORMAN. Now! (*The lower part of NORMAN's face is a mask of red, and his manner is now that of a wild animal.*) Now we'll see! Pincers! (*ANGELA brings him the pincers. The cloth has fallen to the ground, but LUGG's face reveals only exhaustion, and no trace of fear.*) Open! (*LUGG opens his mouth, but as NORMAN approaches him, LUGG jerks his head, and a set of false teeth fall to the ground. NORMAN starts back in disgust. There is a moment's pause, then NORMAN kicks the teeth savagely across the stage.*) Listen to me, animal! *I* am normal! Do you hear? Do you hear? *I* am normal.

LUGG. My poor friend.

NORMAN. Revenge! Revenge! Drill! (*ANGELA fetches him the drill. There is a long bore attached to it, and the whole thing is on the end of a long flex. He switches it on, and there is a whirring sound.*) Now. (*He approaches Lugg.*) This is coming into your brain, Lugg.

LUGG. My poor friend. Do you think I haven't suffered enough?

NORMAN. Suffered? You?

LUGG. All my life! The agonies of the human race. If you kill me, you'll only release me.

NORMAN. You're afraid of me, aren't you? Admit it! You're afraid of me!

LUGG. What is there for me to fear?

NORMAN. Me! This! (*Waving the drill*)

LUGG. I am tired. Come through to my brain, Mr. Norman, come through and release me. (*NORMAN stares at him for a moment, then switches off the drill.*)

NORMAN. (*his voice closer to normal now*) What's wrong with you?

LUGG. I am tired. (*We see that he is sagging in the straps.*)

NORMAN. You're not afraid. How can you rule me from there? (*Long pause; he kneels in front of LUGG.*) Why did you do this to me? Answer me! Why did you do this? Answer! (*LUGG slowly straightens up and focuses his eyes on NORMAN.*)

LUGG. You had tooth-ache.

NORMAN. (*in despair*) Why this? Why this?

LUGG. This is my job, Mr. Norman. To relieve pain. (*NORMAN stands, and looks from LUGG to ANGELA to LUGG.*)

NORMAN. You're mad. Both of you, you're mad. (*He goes to ANGELA, and grips her shoulders.*) Angela. Are you mad? (*He looks into her eyes for a long time, his fingers digging deep into her shoulders. Then slowly his expression relaxes, and gently he takes the coat off her. Keeping his eyes on her all the time, he places the coat on the chair and returns to her.*)

LUGG. No, no! You fool, no! (*NORMAN takes her in his arms and holds her very tightly, kissing her passionately. She remains utterly passive. Quietly:*) Fool, fool! I warned you! I warned you! Oh why is the human race so blind, so closed in by itself? Why must man be his own prisoner, his own slave? Is there no way in which we can get back to grace, no way in which we can destroy the evil. . . .

NORMAN. Be quiet!

LUGG. . . . and the terror we inflict on ourselves? How can . . .

NORMAN. Be quiet, damn you!

LUGG. . . . we stop the hatred, the violence, if those. . . .

NORMAN. Nails! Hammer!

LUGG. . . . who have suffered learn nothing from their pain? (*ANGELA fetches hammer and nails from the cupboard, and gives them to NORMAN, who proceeds to hammer nails into LUGG's body — especially his hands — though we can only see NORMAN's movements. LUGG continues to talk throughout this operation.*) As if the thousands of years meant nothing, as if each generation were the first to tread the earth, and the first to rape and kill, and the first to shed blood and weep over blood that is shed.

NORMAN. Damn you, be quiet!

LUGG. So many of us have tried, but it's like a sea . . .

NORMAN. Can't you feel pain?

LUGG. . . . that smashes down the sand walls, or like a fire that you smother in one place. . . .

NORMAN. Be quiet! Be quiet!

LUGG. . . . only to find it has sprung up all round you.

NORMAN. (*with great blows*) Quiet! Quiet! Quiet!

LUGG. Why must blood be answered with blood? Can we not learn to live together, to be at one with one another, to desire only what is ours, and to give what is ours to others. . . .

NORMAN. Gag! Gag! (*ANGELA brings him a gag.*)

LUGG. . . . so that all may share and live in peace and blessed harmony, never more to. . . . (*The gag is on, and although he continues to talk, we can no longer distinguish words. NORMAN steps back, and we see the "nails" sticking from LUGG's hands.*)

NORMAN. Animal! You can talk till your tongue falls out now! But you can't reach me, do you hear. We can't hear you, animal! Do you think you can destroy other people, and not be made to suffer in return? Do you? Well now you can think again. You've had your last chance, and now you're going to feel it for yourself. Both of you. (*To ANGELA*) Lie down! (*She does.*) You think you can destroy me? Because you disfigure me you think I'm powerless? Do you? (*Shouting*) I'm in command! I'm in command. (*He kneels beside ANGELA.*) I'm going to possess you. And kill him. You hear me! I'm going to kill you, animal! (*To ANGELA*) And I'll take you! Then we'll . . . (*ALICE and a POLICEMAN come through the waiting room, and into the surgery. There is a silence of shock all round.*) Alice! Alice! Oh my God! (*He bursts into tears, going to her, and enfolding her in his arms.*)

POLICEMAN. I'd like to know what's been goin' on here.

NORMAN. Alice, Alice.

POLICEMAN. Stand up, Miss, if you don't mind. (*ANGELA gets up.*)

ALICE. What's been happening? Your mouth is covered in red stuff.

NORMAN. It's blood.

ALICE. No it's not. (*Wiping it*) It's some sort of . . . more like tomato ketchup.

POLICEMAN. (*standing by LUGG*) I think you'd better phone for an ambulance, Miss. Looks like he's unconscious. (*ANGELA goes to the cupboard and brings out the phone.*)

NORMAN. He . . . he . . . he took all my teeth out, Alice. He . . .

ALICE. I came as soon as I . . . But he hasn't!

NORMAN. It's been a nightmare. (*The POLICEMAN releases LUGG, and catches him as he falls.*)

POLICEMAN. Hurry, Miss, please.

ALICE. Did you say he'd taken your teeth out?

NORMAN. It was agony. It was agony!

ALICE. But he hasn't. Your teeth are all there.

ANGELA. Ambulance. 25 Heathfield Road. Thank you. (*The POLICEMAN has lowered LUGG to the floor.*)

POLICEMAN. I shall want a full statement from all of you about this. (*NORMAN feels his mouth with his fingers.*)

NORMAN. But . . . but he took them out. He took them all out, with pincers. (*The POLICEMAN busies himself looking after LUGG.*) He . . . he put them all in the bowl. Angela, bowl. (*ANGELA brings the bowl from the cupboard. Looking into it:*) My God! (*He holds up several nails.*)

NORMAN. Alice, he didn't take them out! He didn't!

POLICEMAN. Now I want to know what's been going on here. Would you mind getting dressed, Miss? (*ANGELA puts her white coat on.*)

ALICE. And so do I. Who is this girl, Norman?

NORMAN. She . . . she's Angela. She's the receptionist. Alice, he didn't take my teeth out!

POLICEMAN. This man has had nails driven into him, and I'd like to know who did it.

NORMAN. (*as if in a daze*) I did it.

ALICE. Norman!

NORMAN. I did it!

POLICEMAN. (*with notebook at the ready*) May I know why, sir?

NORMAN. He . . . he took my teeth out. I . . .

POLICEMAN. Took your teeth out?

ALICE. He didn't, Norman!

NORMAN. (*going to ANGELA, and shaking her violently*) Angela, what's happened? Tell me what's happened!

POLICEMAN. Now then, sir. (*Pulling NORMAN away*) No violence.

NORMAN. Angela! What happened?

ANGELA. You crucified Mr. Lugg, and you tried to rape me.

NORMAN. No, it's not true! He took my teeth out!

ALICE. Norman, he didn't.

POLICEMAN. Just say that again slowly, will you, Miss?

ANGELA. He crucified Mr. Lugg, and he tried to rape me.

NORMAN. It's not true! Alice, you must believe me! It's not true! The man . . . he tortured me. Officer, listen to me. I came in, and . . . he strapped me to that board. Then he tortured me, and . . . he took . . . he pretended to take all my teeth out . . . (*LUGG, looking close to death, has sat up.*)

LUGG. (*in faint voice*) Officer! (*They all turn to listen to him.*)

LUGG. Officer. I tried to help him. I tried to cure him. I . . . I did what I could . . . but it's no use. He's mad. He's quite mad. (*LUGG sinks back.*)

NORMAN. It's not true. (*The POLICEMAN takes his arm.*) It's not true. I'm normal. I'm normal! (*Screaming*) I'm normal!

CURTAIN

THE END

The Escapologist

a play in one act

CHARACTERS

ESCALINI
ELSIE
JOE

SCENE: A street
TIME: The present

The Escapologist

The scene is a street. Present are ESCALINI, middle-aged, semi-cultured, ELSIE, his wife, less cultured, and JOE, a tall negro.

ESCALINI. I'm an escapologist.

ELSIE. 'E's an escapologist.

ESCALINI. I'm an artist in the art of escapology.

ELSIE. Escapology.

ESCALINI. These chains that you see round my feet are solid steel. No tricks, no hanky-panky. Solid steel. Feel 'em. Go on, feel 'em. (*He offers them to the negro, who feels 'em.*) Solid.

ELSIE. Solid.

ESCALINI. Now you can tie me in those chains any way you like. You can bind me up in 'em, and before you can say Open Sesame, I'll be out of 'em.

ELSIE. Out of 'em.

ESCALINI. That's my trade.

ELSIE. It's 'is trade.

ESCALINI. I'm an escapologist you see.

ELSIE. See.

ESCALINI. You may have heard of me. Escalini's the name. The famous Escalini. I don't know what country you come from, sir, but wherever it is, I'll wager they know the name Escalini. I've travelled through the deserts of North Africa, the pampases of South America, the Khyber Pass, the Mysterious Orient, and the . . . er . . . jungles of the Kalahari. The Russias have echoed with applause at the name of Escalini, and the Americas have rocked and rolled in ecstasy at my feats. Escalini.

ELSIE. Lini.

ESCALINI. Name the city, sir, and I'll name you the streets you've walked along.

JOE. Bethlehem. (*Silence*)

ELSIE. 'E said Bethlehem.

ESCALINI. Name any city, sir.

JOE. I name Bethlehem. (*Another silence*)

ESCALINI. Now these chains, sir. You've already examined them, and you must have been struck . . . by the quality . . .

ELSIE. 'E said Bethlehem.

ESCALINI. (*struggling on*) The quality of the steel, sir. Sheffield, sir.

ELSIE. Let's get away from 'ere.

ESCALINI. (*insistent*) Sheffield! A city of steel. Indestructible. The very name shines hard and solid. Sheffield!

JOE. Bethlehem. (*Silence*)

ELSIE. (*to ESCALINI*) I've seen 'im before somewhere. I don't like it. 'E don't come from 'ere.

ESCALINI. I'll speak to him. (*To Joe*) You are a negro. Aren't you?

ELSIE. 'E's a negro.

ESCALINI. What country are you from? Wherever it is, I'll wager I'm known there. Escalini's the name. The Great Escalini. Of course.

JOE. You don't know who I am, do you?

ESCALINI. Who you are? Why should I want to know who you are?

JOE. Why do you tell me your name?

ESCALINI. I tell you my name . . . so that you should know who I am.

JOE. Why should I want to know who you are?

ESCALINI. I am Escalini.

JOE. I am Joe.

ELSIE. Joe.

ESCALINI. I don't wish to know your name.

JOE. But you told me your name.

ESCALINI. My friend. . . .

ELSIE. Careful.

ESCALINI. My acquaintance . . . I have told you my name, because it's a name to be reckoned with. To be remembered. My name matters.

JOE. My name?

ESCALINI. We couldn't care less about your name. *My* name matters. (*To ELSIE*) I've made myself clear, haven't I?

ELSIE. Clear.

JOE. What's an escapologist?

ESCALINI. Ah! Now that's more like it. (*To ELSIE*) These fellows aren't so bad once you get talking to them. An escapologist, my friend, is one who is an expert in the art of escaping.

ELSIE. Caping.

ESCALINI. Now these chains that you see at my feet are solid steel. Made in Sheffield.

ELSIE. Sheffield.

ESCALINI. You can enchain me any way you like, with any knots you like. You can put padlocks on me wherever you like. But before you can say Open Sesame, I'll be free. That's escapology, my friend, the art of escaping.

ELSIE. Caping.

ESCALINI. There's no chains can hold Escalini.

JOE. What do you do once you're free?

ESCALINI. Do?

ELSIE. Do?

ESCALINI. What do you mean, what do I do?

JOE. When you're out of the chains, what comes next?

ESCALINI. When I'm out of the chains, I wait till I get back into them.

JOE. So you get into the chains, out of the chains, then back into them.

ELSIE. Into them.

ESCALINI. And out of them.

ELSIE. Out of them.

ESCALINI. So that I can escape.

JOE. I don't see what's the point of it.

ESCALINI. The point?

ELSIE. Point?

JOE. Why you do it?

ESCALINI. My friend, it's an art. Escapology is an art. I am an artist. That's the point.

ELSIE. Point.

JOE. Is it beautiful?

ESCALINI. Beautiful?

ELSIE. Beaut . . . iful?

ESCALINI. My friend, the sight of Escalini escaping is a sight never to be forgotten. It's a memory that will last forever — that is to say, as long as you can remember. You talk of beauty. A Beethoven symphony, a statue by Michelangelo, a Rembrandt painting, a Shakespeare sonnet, an Escalini escape — all in the same breath, my friend. Why, these chains alone are a thing of beauty. Solid steel — Sheffield steel. Indestructible.

ELSIE. Structible.

ESCALINI. Kings and Queens have marvelled at the beauty of Escalini's escapes. Marble pillars have framed my exploits. Prime Ministers and Presidents have turned their back on the state to pay homage to the feats of Escalini. I don't know what country you come from, sir, but I'll wager the ruler of your land has shaken his head in wonder at the beauty of my work. Name me a palace, sir — any palace in the world — and I'll tell you who painted the pictures on the walls. Name me a theatre, sir — any theatre you like, and I'll tell you whose signatures are on the dressing room walls. Number one dressing room that is, of course. The name of Escalini has been fanfared all over the world, my friend.

ELSIE. Acquaintance.

ESCALINI. Acquaintance.

JOE. But you've never played in Jerusalem, have you? (*Silence*)

ELSIE. Let's gerrout of 'ere. Come on, 'Arry.

JOE. What about in Jerusalem? (*Silence*)

ESCALINI. I've had honours from Kings and Queens. . . .

ELSIE. 'E said Jerusalem!

ESCALINI. . . . Presidents and Prime Ministers.

ELSIE. 'Arry! (*Quietly to ESCALINI*) I don't like the look of 'im. 'E ain't normal. It ain't safe ter talk to 'im.

ESCALINI. He's a customer.

ELSIE. It ain't safe!

ESCALINI. I'll talk to him. (*To JOE*) Now then, sir, have you felt the weight of these chains?

JOE. I've felt them.

ESCALINI. The solidity?

JOE. I've had them in my hands.

ESCALINI. Oh! Well, what do you think of them?

JOE. They're chains, like any other chains.

ESCALINI. Like any other chains! Like any other! My dear sir, these chains are unique! Unique!

ELSIE. 'Arry, let's get out of 'ere.

ESCALINI. There are no chains like these chains.

JOE. Only because they're yours — but I've seen plenty of chains like these.

ESCALINI. Never. Never. These are solid steel. Sheffield steel.

ELSIE. 'Arry.

ESCALINI. Sheffield! (*He looks defiantly at her.*)

ELSIE. (*grudgingly*) Sheffield.

ESCALINI. Now then, sir, I'm not going to beat about the bush with you any more. You've seen these magnificent chains, you've felt their weight, you know their value. If you would care to take them in your hands and to wind them about my person, and then to fasten them with this padlock, which you are perfectly free to examine, I will then astound you, as I have astounded people all over the world, including Kings and Queens, Presidents and Prime Ministers, by releasing myself from them in the twinkling of an eye.

JOE. You want me to tie you up in those chains.

ESCALINI. Exactly. (*To ELSIE*) You see, he's understood.

ELSIE. I don't like it.

JOE. Supposing you can't get out of them?

ESCALINI. Can't get out of them? Escalini can't get out of these chains? Ho, ho, my friend — that's like saying supposing the sun doesn't rise tomorrow! Except I suppose that could happen. Escalini never fails, my friend.

JOE. But you've never been tied up by me before, have you?

ESCALINI. That's true. Escalini never forgets a face, and I'm quite sure I've never been tied up by you.

ELSIE. Up by you.

JOE. Then what make, you so sure you can escape if *I* tie you up?

ESCALINI. Ah, I see. I see the point of your question. You think that I only escape if an accomplice ties me up. Let me reassure you, Escalini has no accomplices. My wife accompanies me, it's true, but she plays no part in my act — she's only there to collect any offerings and to show that I'm normal.

ELSIE. Normal.

ESCALINI. It is always a member of the audience who ties me up.

JOE. If I tie you up, you won't be able to escape.

ESCALINI. Ha, ha, do you hear that, Elsie? The gentleman thinks I shan't be able to escape. Come along now, sir, I'll take the risk.

JOE. What about your wife?

ESCALINI. What about her?

JOE. Do you want her tied up too?

ESCALINI. Oh no, we don't normally. . . . but wait a moment, that might add to the attraction of my act. If the two of us were tied up together, it might well enhance the impressiveness of the spectacle.

ELSIE. I ain't gointer be tied up. . . .

ESCALINI. Come, Elsie, let's see what this does for us.

ELSIE. No.

ESCALINI. (*very hard*) Elsie!

ELSIE. (*submitting*) Elsie. (*They stand together.*)

ESCALINI. Back to back, I think, Elsie.

JOE. That's right, back to back, so you can't see each other.

ESCALINI. We are ready. (*JOE winds the chain round them, occasionally giving it a complicated twist.*) Tight as you like. Escalini can take it.

ELSIE. 'Is wife can't.

ESCALINI. Then you padlock it — if you're quite satisfied.

JOE. I'm satisfied. (*He padlocks it.*)

ESCALINI. Now ladies and gentlemen, you can all see that Escalini and his wife are firmly imprisoned by these chains, these solid Sheffield chains.

ELSIE. Sheffield chains.

ESCALINI. The padlock has been fastened — made in Birmingham incidentally — and the key is in the hand of this kind gentleman, our gaoler, ha, ha. There can be no doubt that we are well and truly bound up. And yet I, Escalini, the greatest escapologist the world has ever seen, will, without the use of my arms, without the use of my legs, but using nothing except my brain and my art, I, Escalini, will now astound you all by removing these chains in the twinkling of an eye. Are we ready? One, two, two and a half. . . . THREE! (*He gives an elaborate twist-jerk-shake, and remains as firmly enchained as before.*)

ELSIE. Three.

ESCALINI. Ayaaa! (*With this cry he repeats the movement, rather more energetically. Same result.*)

ELSIE. (*deadpan*) Ayaaa!

ESCALINI. I see. Yes. Clever, but. . . . (*strain*). . . . not clever enough! (*Heave, jerk, shake. No good.*)

ELSIE. Clever enough.

ESCALINI. (*now shaking with desperate violence*) Grrrrrrrrrr-rrrrrrrrrr! (*Eventually he stops, exhausted.*)

ELSIE. Grrr.

JOE. You seem to be having trouble. (*ESCALINI looks at him balefully.*)

JOE. I warned you. (*ESCALINI starts struggling again, but soon gives up.*) I'll let you out if you like.

ESCALINI. I am Escalini.

ELSIE. Lini.

ESCALINI. ESCALINI!

JOE. I don't mind if you want to stay there — it's your choice. At least it'll save you the bother of finding other people to tie you up.

ESCALINI. I'll get out of it. You'll see.

ELSIE. See.

ESCALINI. No chains can hold Escalini.

ELSIE. Lini.

ESCALINI. I'll find the way out.

JOE. Only by dying. (*Silence*)

ELSIE. 'E said dyin'.

ESCALINI. No chains can hold Escalini.

JOE. These'll hold you till you die. (*Another silence*)

ESCALINI. Kings and Queens, Presidents. . . .

ELSIE. (*very distressed*) 'E said dyin'! 'Arry!

ESCALINI. Presidents and Prime Ministers. . . . have all seen. . . .

ELSIE. Dyin', 'Arry!

ESCALINI. Have all seen the great Escalini, and marvelled at his feats! There are no chains on earth that can hold him.

JOE. There are no chains on earth that can hold anyone once they're dead. (*Silence*)

ELSIE. 'Arry, tell 'im to unlock us. I'm scared.

ESCALINI. There's nothing to be scared of. Nothing. I'll talk to him. (*To JOE*) You're a negro, aren't you? I've been to your country. I know it well. The King is a personal friend of mine, as a matter of fact.

JOE. Do you want me to unlock you?

ESCALINI. There are very few countries that I haven't been to — very few. I've appeared in most of the great cities of the world. I know all the main streets, all the theatres, all the palaces.

JOE. What about the churches? (*Short silence*)

ESCALINI. All the streets, all the theatres. . . .

JOE. And the graveyards?

ELSIE. (*shouting*) Tell 'im to unlock us! 'Arry! (*Short silence*)

ESCALINI. I am the great Escalini. I have appeared in all the major cities of the world. . . .

JOE. I'm not staying with you for the rest of time, you know. I'll let you have the key, but if you don't want it, I'll be on my way. Now, do you want me to set you free? (*Pause*)

ESCALINI. I'll set myself free.

JOE. Then what shall I do with the key?

ESCALINI. Throw it away.

ELSIE. 'Arry!

ESCALINI. Throw it away!

ELSIE. What you doin'?

ESCALINI. I said to throw it away! Do you hear? Away!

ELSIE. (*defeated*) Away.

ESCALINI. The great Escalini has never needed a key to get him out of his chains.

ELSIE. Chains.

ESCALINI. I am a human being, not an animal. Throw the key away. And marvel at the majesty of Escalini, who defies the force that would defeat all other men. I shall escape, without help, from these chains.

ELSIE. Chains.

ESCALINI. I am Escalini.

ELSIE. Lini.

JOE. I'm going.

ESCALINI. Wait!

ELSIE. Wait! (*JOE waits.*)

ESCALINI. You can't leave us like this.

JOE. If you want me to set you free, I'll set you free, but you must make up your mind.

ESCALINI. I'm in a dilemma. You don't understand my position.

JOE. We all have our problems.

ESCALINI. Not like mine. No-one's ever had a problem like this before. Can I talk to you? You're a negro, aren't you? You come from a different part of the world. I know you. . . .

JOE. Do you want me to set you free, or are you going to stay there till you die? (*Silence*)

ELSIE. 'Arry, tell 'im to let us go. . . .

ESCALINI. I am an escapologist. . . .

JOE. Stick to the subject, will you?

ELSIE. 'Arry, please!

ESCALINI. (*To ELSIE*) What is it?

ELSIE. 'Arry, if yer can't get us out, tell 'im to unlock us. I don't like it 'ere. I ain't comfortable.

ESCALINI. There's plenty of people worse off than you.

ELSIE. I know. But that don't 'elp. Tell 'im to undo us.

ESCALINI. Half the world is starving. Keep that thought in your mind before you start complaining.

ELSIE. 'Arry, ask 'im to undo the chains.

ESCALINI. I'll talk to him. (*To JOE*) You spoke just now of Bethlehem, and Jerusalem.

ELSIE. Oh Gawd!

ESCALINI. I've heard a good deal about these places, but never had the good fortune to play there. I've always been interested in religion. Are you a religious man? I believe that God is in a man's heart, you know. It sickens me to hear people talk as if God was only to be contacted in church. Don't you agree? But there are certain problems I could never find the answer to. For instance, if God is perfect and also all-powerful, and in the beginning there was only God, then how does evil come about? Fascinating, isn't it? I've thought about that for hours. And what about this for a conundrum: if a man has free will, but God knows everything, then God must have known in advance that man would choose the wrong thing — and if God knew this in advance, then how can it be said man has free will? You see what I'm driving at, don't you? I find this sort of thing fascinating, don't you? Fascinating.

JOE. When you die, when your eyes stop seeing and your heart stops beating and your bones are buried in the earth, what's going to become of you?

ELSIE. 'Arry, fer Gawd's sake, let 'im undo us!

ESCALINI. My friend. . . . have you ever been to Sheffield? A city of steel, Sheffield, solid as these chains. There are some towns. . . .

JOE. If you like, I'll set your wife free, but you'll have to make up your mind quickly. (*Short pause*)

ELSIE. 'Arry. 'Arry, 'e said 'e'd set me free.

JOE. (*going round to her*) What about it?

ELSIE. Well, I dunno. 'Arry?

ESCALINI. What is it?

ELSIE. 'E said 'e'd set me free.

ESCALINI. You want to leave me?

ELSIE. 'Arry, I ain't comfortable!

ESCALINI. So that's it! That's it! A moment of discomfort, and you're ready to break up the home! This is the female attitude to marriage, is it? You'll go round collecting the money, won't you? You'll eat the food I earn for us, won't you? You'll wear the clothes I buy with the sweat of my labours. But an instant of pain, and you're prepared to leave me to suffer on my own! When all is well, the help-mate is by your side, smiling and affectionate. But at the first sign of trouble, she's away, and you can die like a dog on your own.

ELSIE. I never said I'd leave yer, 'Arry.

ESCALINI. This is what you get when you treat a woman well. (*Twisting round to see JOE*) It's all your fault. We were perfectly happy till you came along, with all your talk of God and religion. Welcome a stranger into your house, and when your back's turned, he's stealing your wife. To hell with you all!

JOE. I'll undo you as well, if you want me to.

ESCALINI. I won't listen. Get thee behind me, Satan! When I think of all the great Kings and Queens that have paid homage to me — and now I've sunk this low. I writhe in horror.

JOE. (*to ELSIE*) Shall I undo you?

ELSIE. You'd better not.

JOE. Then I'll be on my way.

ESCALINI. Wait! Wait! Don't do anything hasty. This thing has to be discussed.

JOE. (*going to him*) There's nothing to be discussed. If you've decided to stay here, then you can stay here. I've got my own life to lead.

ESCALINI. What shall I do? What shall I do? If you unlock us. I'm a failure. If you leave us, we're stuck.

JOE. Make up your mind. (*Pause*)

ESCALINI. I'll tell you something. I have no colour prejudice. Isn't that a wonderful thing? I saw straight away that you were a negro, and yet it made no difference. After all, you're just as human as I am, aren't you? I have many coloured friends. They regard me as a brother.

ELSIE. I've 'ad enough. Undo me. (*JOE goes round to her.*)

ESCALINI. Elsie, you can't! (*He begins to struggle violently.*)

ELSIE. I ain't stayin' all chained up like a monkey all me life.

ESCALINI. You can't! I forbid it! (*JOE is setting her free.*) This is against the law! I won't have it! You'll be punished! Stop this at once! Do you hear? (*She is free.*)

ELSIE. (*to JOE*) Thanks very much. (*To ESCALINI*) I'm out. (*ESCALINI fights to get free, but soon gives up.*)

ESCALINI. (*to ELSIE*) Traitor. (*He spits on the ground.*)

ELSIE. (*still getting back the circulation*) Don't be so stupid. 'E'll let you out too.

ESCALINI. I still have some pride! I'm not an animal! I'm Escalini. (*Shouting at her*) Escalini!

ELSIE. (*contemptuously*) Lini.

ESCALINI. (*to JOE*) You think you can scare me with your talk of bones, and churches. Well, nothing scares Escalini. Nothing! I'll argue with the best of you, and I'll beat you. I know what matters in this world. You can't scare me. If you're so clever, see if you can get out of chains like these! Feel them. Go on, feel them! Solid! Steel! There's nothing more real than these, my friend. To hell with you! (*Normal, matter-of-fact voice:*) Could you just loosen this one around my throat — it's throttling me. (*JOE loosens it.*) Thanks. What was I saying? Ah! (*Back to rant:*) To hell with you! You can't scare me!

JOE. (*to ELSIE*) I'll leave the key with you. (*Making a move*)

ESCALINI. Wait! Wait, wait, wait, wait. You can't go yet. Not until you've made a contribution.

JOE. A contribution to what?

ESCALINI. My dear friend, I have to live. You've watched my performance, which I've given you free of charge — what else do you want — my death? (*Silence*)

ELSIE. 'Arry!

ESCALINI. (*almost in a trance*) Death!

ELSIE. 'Arry, stop it!

ESCALINI. Bones. Worms. The sockets of the eyes . . .

ELSIE. (*to JOE*) 'Elp us. (*Back to ESCALINI*) 'Arry! Pack it in! (*Slapping his face*) Think about yer chains, 'Arry. Yer chains, 'Arry. Sheffield. Solid steel. Sheffield.

ESCALINI. The last trumpet. The sheep and the goats. Down . . .

ELSIE. 'Arry!

JOE. He'll be a good Christian yet!

ESCALINI. . . . in flames. The eternal cremation.

ELSIE. Stop it for Gawd's sake!

JOE. Why stop it? Let him come to terms with it.

ELSIE. Give us some money, quick.

ESCALINI. I plead guilty.

JOE. But I've only. . . .

ELSIE. Quick! (*JOE gives her a note.*) 'Ere, 'Arry. Look! (*She holds it in front of his eyes.*) Lolly, 'Arry. Lolly. (*Gradually his eyes focus on the money.*) Lovely lolly. Fer 'Arry.

ESCALINI. (*coming round*) Well, this is very handsome of you, sir. Very handsome indeed. Not that the performance isn't worth it, but there are few people around today who really appreciate art.

JOE. I didn't intend . . .

ESCALINI. No, no, sir, not another word. Your contribution speaks for itself. These are hard times for us artists, with the inflation and the violence, but one person like yourself makes it all worthwhile.

ELSIE. Worthwhile. (*She is now at his side, reunited.*)

ESCALINI. It's moments like this that stand out in the memory.

The tickertape in New York, the Wembley roar, crowds lining the Champs-Elysees. I've travelled the world with my act, you know. There's scarcely a city I haven't been to — haven't taken by storm. Escalini is known everywhere, a household word. The man no chains can hold.

JOE. But you're still in my chains.

ESCALINI. From the Gobi Desert to the Arctic Circle my feats are renowned. The Entertainer Supreme.

ELSIE. Supreme.

ESCALINI. The Artist Supreme.

ELSIE. Supreme.

ESCALINI. The quintessence of human ingenuity.

ELSIE. (*looking sharply at him*) Uity.

ESCALINI. So long as the earth holds Escalini, Escalini holds the earth. Not even God could tie a knot to keep me.

ELSIE. Keep me.

JOE. But you're still trapped! (*ESCALINI looks almost mockingly at him, then with the gentlest of shrugs, frees himself from the chains, which fall around his feet.*)

ELSIE. Thank Gawd, I thought yer'd 'ad it!

ESCALINI. Not even God, my friend. Escalini is supreme.

ELSIE. (*looking at him with admiration*) Supreme.

CURTAIN

THE END

The Death Artist

a play in one act

CHARACTERS

THE VICTIM, in his sixties
THE DEATH ARTIST, in his thirties

SCENE: The Victim's counting-house
TIME: The present

THE DEATH ARTIST was first performed by the Theater-gruppe der Universitat Konstanz, West Germany, on May 3rd 1973, directed by the author.

The Death Artist

The VICTIM sits at a table in mid-stage, confronted by piles of money. The corners of the stage are in darkness. There is no other furniture, no door visible, and no window.

VICTIM. (*counting banknotes*) Nine hundred and ninety-nine thousand nine hundred and ninety-seven. Nine hundred and ninety-nine thousand nine hundred and ninety-eight. Nine hundred and ninety-nine thousand nine hundred and ninety-nine. Heh heh heh heh! Heh heh heeeh! Heh heh heeeeeh! A MILLION! A MILLI-MILLI-MILLION! Ahahahaaaaaaaaaa! MILLION! I . . . have . . . a . . . million. Hoho, a million. I must let the Queen know about this. (*He reflects.*) No, better not — she might want to borrow some. Best to keep these things quiet. Mouse-like . . . with a million. (*Shouting*) I'm rich! (*Whispering*) I'm rich. And not even the Inland Revenue knows about it. Nobody knows about it. (*The ARTIST emerges from the far right-hand corner of the stage, but stays behind the VICTIM.*) Unless . . . . there's been a miscount. A slip-up over one of the million hurdles. One must be certain. One must check. All great men are thorough. One, two, three, four, etc. (*The ARTIST walks to the front of the stage, staying on the right-hand side and ignoring the VICTIM. The latter looks up in mid-count, and is horrified.*) Who . . . who are you? Who are you? What do you want, eh? There's no. . . . (*He throws a cover over the money, his movements jerky with panic.*) . . . there's no money here, you know. No money. You won't get a penny out of me! Now, you go away! How did you get in? Who are you? What? What?

ARTIST. There's no need to shout.

VICTIM. How did you get in here? Nobody can get in here. Not even I can get in here. . . . sometimes. . . .

ARTIST. I got in, that's all.

VICTIM. What do you want? I've got no money. I'm a poor man. Nothing. Nothing, nothing at all to my name. The clothes I stand up in. And they're on hire purchase. I'm behind in the instalments. They'll be taking the jacket next week — I'll show you the letter.

39

ARTIST. I don't want your money.

VICTIM. What money? I haven't got any money!

ARTIST. I'm not interested.

VICTIM. Not interested? Not interested in money? (*Calming down*) Oh! Good, good. I haven't any, you see.

ARTIST. This is a peculiar place, isn't it?

VICTIM. Peculiar? Peculiar?

ARTIST. No doors. No windows. Afraid of people coming, in are you?

VICTIM. People? What sort of people?

ARTIST. Any sort.

VICTIM. I don't know any people!

ARTIST. There's no need to be aggressive. It was a civil question.

VICTIM. Who are you? What do you want?

ARTIST. I've been given a job.

VICTIM. What job? How did you get in here? I. . . . I demand to know. This. . . . this is my home — such as it is. Very bare, as you see. How did you get in?

ARTIST. I walked in.

VICTIM. You can't. This place is sealed.

ARTIST. Every place is sealed, one way or another. You all think you're inviolable.

VICTIM. What sort of a job? You said you'd been given. . . .

ARTIST. Given a job. For what it's worth, you're the job.

VICTIM. Me? Me? You're wasting your time. There's no money in here. . . .

ARTIST. Your life, not your money.

VICTIM. What? What did you say?

ARTIST. I've got to kill you.

VICTIM. (*after pause*) Me? Did you say . . . . kill. . . . me?

ARTIST. I have to put an end to your existence, if you want the posh terminology. I have to enable you to 'pass on', to 'depart' to sever your connections.

VICTIM. I . . . I . . . I . . . I don't even know you.

ARTIST. That's not necessary. It's a one-way process.

VICTIM. Um. . . . a one-way process?

ARTIST. I kill you.

VICTIM. (*after pause*) Is it a joke?

ARTIST. No.

VICTIM. Look. . . . um . . . young man . . . I . . . er . . . I do have . . . just a little money. A few pounds. I . . .

ARTIST. Have you any ideas yourself?

VICTIM. I beg your pardon?

ARTIST. How it's to be done.

VICTIM. How what's to be done?

ARTIST. Your. . . . decease.

VICTIM. My . . . ?

ARTIST. Your death.

VICTIM. Look, young man . . . supposing I say. . . . um . . . five pounds, eh? You can do a lot with five pounds . . .

ARTIST. Are you trying to buy me off?

VICTIM. Pardon?

ARTIST. I thought people like you finished in the Middle Ages! Five pounds, eh?

VICTIM. Well. . . . perhaps I can manage a little bit more.

ARTIST. (*serious*) You're going to die. You can't buy your way out of it. The question is *how* you're going to die. You look very healthy.

VICTIM. (*after slight pause*) I. . . . I could raise . . . probably . . . a fairly large sum. . . . fairly substantial. I have some influential friends. . . . I might. . . . um. . . . need a little bit of time. . . . a hundred. . . . perhaps? Or I may even be able to squeeze some. . . .

ARTIST. Supposing I were to smother you in money? Bury you alive in banknotes? It would be original, wouldn't it? And appropriate. But then you haven't got enough, have you? You're not really rich enough.

VICTIM. I'm a million. . . . no. No, no—I have no money. Young man, are you serious about killing me? Maybe I'm foolish, but. . . . I can't help wondering. I'm just a defenceless old man, you know, and . . . well. . . .

ARTIST. If it'll set your mind at rest, I'll say it again. I'm going to kill you.

VICTIM. But why?

ARTIST. Does there have to be a reason?

VICTIM. I've not done you any harm. Have I?

ARTIST. (*slowly*) You've reached the end of your span.

VICTIM. But I'm . . . I'm quite willing to come to terms . . .

ARTIST. Good. Resignation's always a welcome attitude. Leaves me free to get on with the job.

VICTIM. I didn't mean that. I meant . . . a price.

ARTIST. Look, I'm a very patient man. I take a pride in my work, and I don't like unpleasant scenes, so will you get this into your head before my patience runs out? You're going to be killed. Money is irrelevant in your situation. Is that clear?

VICTIM. (*cowed*) Yes. Yes, sir. . . . I . . . I understand. You . . . you've made it very clear. Might I . . . might I just ask one question? Um . . . who . . . who is it . . . that wants me killed?

ARTIST. Nobody wants you killed.

VICTIM. (*after pause*) But . . . but if nobody wants me killed . . . why? I mean . . . why kill me?

ARTIST. Do you think the sun comes up in the morning for your benefit?

VICTIM. (*not understanding*) No.

ARTIST. Before it rains, are you consulted?

VICTIM. No.

ARTIST. That is the situation you're in. You're faced with a fact — that's all. And the fact is that you're to be killed, and eaten.

VICTIM. Eaten!

ARTIST. Devoured and digested.

VICTIM. Young man, you're . . . you're really frightening me now. I . . . I don't mind admitting it, I'm . . . I'm frightened. You're a very persuasive speaker. But this . . . this is beyond acceptance. That sort of thing isn't done . . . not any more.

ARTIST. As you like.

VICTIM. It died out . . . years ago. Even in primitive countries.

ARTIST. Well then you'll be the lucky one to revive the old custom, won't you?

VICTIM. No, no, you're going too far. Now . . . now I know this is just a joke. You . . . you have a very strange sense of humour, but I suppose it's just . . . part of your generation. I never could understand young people's jokes, but . . . hahaha . . . yes, you. . . . you did have me worried. (*Pause. The ARTIST looks at him without a glimmer of a smile.*) It . . . it *is* a joke.

ARTIST. Killed and eaten. The problem is . . . how? I must say there's something tricky about you. I can't quite see why you should have been assigned to me. Unless it's for the challenge.

VICTIM. May I ask . . . who is going to eat me?

ARTIST. Who usually eats people when they're dead? Don't ask stupid questions.

VICTIM. But look . . . I . . . I'm . . . I'm very thin. I'll not make a good meal at all. I'm just a bag of bones really.

ARTIST. I expect they'll find some flesh on you somewhere.

VICTIM. There must be plenty of other people . . . fatter . . . than me. (*The ARTIST silences him with a look. Pause.*)

ARTIST. Apart from money, what are your interests?

VICTIM. Well . . . (*in difficulties*) . . . well . . . I haven't many interests.

ARTIST. Have you *any* interests?

VICTIM. No.

ARTIST. How would you *like* to die?

VICTIM. I . . . I've not thought about it.

ARTIST. Well you should have done! A man of your age should have thought about it and worked something out!

VICTIM. (*cowed*) Well . . . I . . . I'd like to die peacefully . . . in my bed . . . without pain. Just . . . dropping off.

ARTIST. That's not much help.

VICTIM. I wouldn't like to suffer.

ARTIST. Nobody wants to suffer. But you can't expect *me* to let you drop off in bed.

VICTIM. Can't we . . . er . . . postpone it then? Till we . . . find a solution.

ARTIST. That's a real stroke of inspiration, that is. A very original thought. And I wonder what your motives might be. I happen to be working against a time limit.

VICTIM. A time limit?

ARTIST. A limitation—as regards time. Your time, as they say, is limited. There is a limit beyond which you will not be allowed to live. Clear?

VICTIM. How . . . how long is this time limit?

ARTIST. That's a professional secret. What sort of death are you most afraid of?

VICTIM. Well . . . anything that makes me suffer. I . . . I shouldn't like to be eaten by a crocodile.

ARTIST. You're scarcely likely to be eaten by a crocodile in the heart of London, are you?

VICTIM. There's the zoo.

ARTIST. Do you ever go to the zoo?

VICTIM. No.

ARTIST. Then stick to probabilities, will you?

VICTIM. I . . . I shouldn't like to be eaten by cannibals.

ARTIST. There aren't many of those in London either.

VICTIM. But I thought you said I was going to be . . .

ARTIST. Your death has to be natural—that is to say, plausible. Much as you may dread being chewed up by a crocodile, or boiled in a pot with a sprig of parsley in your ear, such a death is not within the realms of probability, and therefore it doesn't enter into consideration. What *plausible* death are you afraid of?

VICTIM. Well . . . a slow and painful poisoning?

ARTIST. By whom?

VICTIM. Oh, I . . . I thought *you* were . . .

ARTIST. You don't think I'm going to murder you, do you?

VICTIM. You aren't? (*Hopeful*) You mean . . . it *was* a joke?

ARTIST. Oh give me patience!

VICTIM. It wasn't.

ARTIST. You are going to die. I have to find a way of killing you. That is the situation.

VICTIM. And the eating?

ARTIST. The eating comes afterwards.

VICTIM. I see. Well if . . . if that's the situation, why . . . why don't you just kill me and have done with it? Why . . . why must you play about with me?

ARTIST. I'm not playing about with you. I'm trying to find a way of killing you. I'm an artist, not a butcher. That's why you've been given to me — though I can't see why you should be singled out. Except that you're difficult.

VICTIM. What do you mean, difficult?

ARTIST. Difficult. Hard to fit in. You tax the imagination.

VICTIM. I don't see why I should be called difficult.

ARTIST. Well let's say you're difficult for somebody like me. Dead easy to do a botched up job — but I'm not like that, you see. I like to do it creatively, artistically.

VICTIM. You're going to arrange an accident, are you?

ARTIST. Possibly.

VICTIM. Well I haven't got a car, and I don't go out. Everybody'll know it was murder. You'll never get away with it.

ARTIST. You tax the imagination.

VICTIM. You'll never get away with it. (*The ARTIST whips the cover off the banknotes, despite a despairing lunge by the VICTIM.*)

ARTIST. Supposing these notes were to catch fire?

VICTIM. Don't! Oh. . . . these are. . . . these are. . . . they're forgeries.

ARTIST. And you were burned up with them?

VICTIM. They're worth nothing. Burned? Did you say burned?

ARTIST. The place is sealed in. You needn't even be burned — just suffocated. Lack of oxygen.

VICTIM. You can't. . . . you can't burn these!

ARTIST. Asbestos, are they?

VICTIM. If you burn them. . . . you'll be suffocated too. If I can't breathe, you can't!

ARTIST. I got in here all right. I expect I can get out again.

VICTIM. And what's to stop me from getting out?

ARTIST. The same thing that's stopped you for sixty years. You live here.

VICTIM. I *can* get out.

ARTIST. In theory.

VICTIM. If the place catches fire, I can get out! I can get out!

ARTIST. In theory. But in practice, you wouldn't, would you?

VICTIM. If my life is in danger, I will! This method of yours won't work.

ARTIST. But supposing I influence you to stay?

VICTIM. Then you'll die as well. You'll have to *be* here to keep me here. If you use violence on me, then they'll find it out. They'll know I've been murdered.

ARTIST. I've no objection to being here with you.

VICTIM. You're mad! You want to kill me and yourself as well? What for?

ARTIST. Who said anything about killing me?

VICTIM. If you stay, *you'll* be suffocated.

ARTIST. I don't need air.

VICTIM. What do you mean?

ARTIST. It should be plain enough. I don't need air. Have a look. (*He pulls down his collar to show the VICTIM his neck.*) Nasty, isn't it? So you see, I don't need air.

VICTIM. (*hoarse with horror*) What are you?

ARTIST. I'm an artist. My colleagues, of course, would probably fix you up with a heart attack, or a cancer, or something like that. But it's not my way. I don't deal in clichés, you see. My way has to be new—original. That's what makes me an artist, as opposed to an artisan. You see the difference?

VICTIM. (*standing up*) I'm going to leave here.

ARTIST. You can't. You're too late. You should have left here years ago, when there was still time. You're out of time now.

VICTIM. I'm going.

ARTIST. If you can find the door. (*The VICTIM looks around.*)

VICTIM. There *is* a door.

ARTIST. Find it.

VICTIM. (*knocking on the wall*) There *is* a door. I know there's a door.

ARTIST. When did you last see it?

VICTIM. I've seen it. It's always been there.

ARTIST. Suddenly disappeared, has it?

VICTIM. (*trying elsewhere*) There *is* a door. You must have come in through a door.

ARTIST. Yes, I'll admit that.

VICTIM. Then I can find it.

ARTIST. Not till my work's over, you can't.

VICTIM. There *is* a door. (*He continues to knock on the wall.*)

ARTIST. All in good time. (*He sits at the desk.*) I was in the same position as you once. Locked in. It's a stupid position to be in, when you think back – but at the time, you don't see it. You're there, and that's you. I said I wanted to get out, but it was too late. They gave me. . . . what you saw. In some ways, I suppose I'm still in that room. Perhaps it was right all the time . . . except I remember how I felt – when I wanted to leave. You won't find that door. It's rusted over. Welded with age. No, I don't think I presented much of a problem in my day. It was all traced out. Straightforward job. Not like you.

VICTIM. Who sent you?

ARTIST. You know who sent me. (*Tension building up again.*)

VICTIM. Tell him I'm not ready.

ARTIST. You should have been ready.

VICTIM. I need more time.

ARTIST. You should always have been ready.

VICTIM. I need more time! I need more time!

ARTIST. For what? Counting?

VICTIM. (*after pause*) Are you going to set fire to them?

ARTIST. It's an idea. Though you're a non-smoker, aren't you?

VICTIM. Yes.

ARTIST. You see? Difficult.

VICTIM. What will you do if. . . . the time limit expires, and you haven't found a way?

ARTIST. There's no danger of that. I always find a way. You won't leave this room alive – that's the one thing you can be certain of. Have you made a will?

VICTIM. No.

ARTIST. Why not? You want the government to take the lot?

VICTIM. I don't want anyone to have my money.

ARTIST. What do you want to do with it, then?

VICTIM. I. . . . I want it to come with me.

ARTIST. To be buried with you?

VICTIM. Yes.

ARTIST. What for?

VICTIM. Because I want it. Perhaps just an announcement in The Times to say how much I left. And all of it to come with me.

ARTIST. You realize it'll disintegrate.

VICTIM. It won't.

ARTIST. Of course it will. Even faster than you.

VICTIM. No.

ARTIST. It will. That stuff's not a millionth as durable as bone. Where's your intelligence?

VICTIM. This is durable.

ARTIST. It's paper. (*He tears up a note.*)

VICTIM. Oh!

ARTIST. That's how durable it is.

VICTIM. Leave it alone! That's my property.

ARTIST. You haven't got any property.

VICTIM. Leave it! This is mine!

ARTIST. Give it to a charity.

VICTIM. It's coming with me.

ARTIST. To starving children.

VICTIM. No.

ARTIST. Blind babies.

VICTIM. No.

ARTIST. The old and insecure.

VICTIM. No.

ARTIST. Why not?

VICTIM. They don't exist! It's all a bluff! They don't exist!

ARTIST. So that's what you are, is it?

VICTIM. What do you mean?

ARTIST. That's what you are. (*He stands up.*) Now I know. It's a lesson I should have learned a long time ago. Not to doubt, but just to find out why.

VICTIM. I don't understand.

ARTIST. Why you were given to me. Now I know. All right!

VICTIM. (*frightened*) What are you going to do?

ARTIST. I'm going to establish a few facts. About existence. First of all, you were looking for the door, weren't you?

VICTIM. The door?

ARTIST. The way out of this room. (*He crosses to the far right-hand corner.*) It's here. Here's the door. And it's unlocked. You can go out.

VICTIM. There. . . . there's no door there.

ARTIST. I'll open it for you. (*Dimly in the shadow, the door opens.*) Just go through it.

VICTIM. I . . . I can't see any door.

ARTIST. Then come closer.

VICTIM. No.

ARTIST. Do you know what's outside this door?

VICTIM. There's nothing. There's no door, and there. . . . there's nothing. (*The ARTIST returns to the VICTIM, coming very close.*)

ARTIST. Out there is pain. Out there are swollen tongues, lepers, tormented minds, stunted limbs, walking bones, and children that are so weak they can't flick the flies away. And you tell me there's no door? Out there is darkness blacker than the darkness you're going to. And you say no door? Out there are people who would call me Saviour! Why don't you go and see them? Beyond the door. (*He crosses the room again and slams the door shut.*) I take back what I said a minute ago. You deserve me. You've been singled out with good reason.

VICTIM. I. . . . I didn't mean what I said. You know that I. . . .I was looking for the door myself. I need more time, thât's all.

ARTIST. Did nobody ever knock at your door?

VICTIM. I. . . . I. . . . knock?

ARTIST. Bang, bang, on the door.

VICTIM. I don't remember hearing anybody.

ARTIST. If somebody knocked on your door, would you answer it?

VICTIM. Yes, yes, of course. (*Loud knocking*)

ARTIST. Answer it. (*The VICTIM goes hesitantly towards the door.*) Answer it!

VICTIM. I. . . . I don't know how to.

ARTIST. By pulling it open.

VICTIM. There's no handle. (*Pause. The VICTIM turns to face the ARTIST. The knocking stops.*) I can't help being what I am.

ARTIST. I'm not your judge.

VICTIM. The knocking's stopped.

ARTIST. They died.

VICTIM. I'm not to be blamed. My father was a drunkard. We lived in poverty.

ARTIST. Who made your father a drunkard?

VICTIM. He. . . . he was not to be blamed.

ARTIST. Who made your father's father a sadist? Who made your father's mother a whore? How far back do you want to go? Who made me a murderer?

VICTIM. None of us can be blamed.

ARTIST. We're all wound up like clockwork, is that it? Well, somebody knows better than you. And that's why you were singled out. . . .

VICTIM. I can't be blamed.

ARTIST. . . . to be dealt with by me. And if it involves suffering, so much the better.

VICTIM. I haven't done anything wrong.

ARTIST. And you haven't done anything right. You're a sinner by omission.

VICTIM. I don't see why you should want to make me suffer.

ARTIST. I want to *make* you suffer, so that I can *let* you suffer.

VICTIM. I've not done anyone any harm. I. . . . I had an unhappy childhood. I. . . . I couldn't be involved. I kept myself to myself. I've not done any harm.

ARTIST. Do you remember what's outside?

VICTIM. (*after slight pause*) Yes.

ARTIST. Do you ever dream about it?

VICTIM. I stopped dreaming. A long time ago.

ARTIST. You're a liar.

VICTIM. I. . . . I'm not responsible for my dreams. . . .

ARTIST. According to you, you're not responsible for anything!

VICTIM. I. . . . One can't believe dreams.

ARTIST. Do you know what I see in my dreams? Eyes. Like yours. Frightened. Men's eyes, women's eyes, children's. Who's responsible for those eyes?

VICTIM. Why. . . . why don't *you* change?

ARTIST. Because there's a use for me as I am. Because now I'm an instrument.

VICTIM. If you keep dreaming of eyes. . . .

ARTIST. They're not sinners' eyes. You're afraid because you've understood. But the eyes I dream of don't understand.

VICTIM. Nevertheless you could change. You could make up for what you've done. . . .

ARTIST. You're not trying to convert me, are you? You are! Well, well! You'll try anything, won't you? What about threatening me? That would be another angle.

VICTIM. How can I threaten you?

ARTIST. Tell me to get out. This is your house. I'm trespassing. You'll send for the police. Won't you try that one? (*The VICTIM is now visibly drained of hope.*)

VICTIM. There's no point in my threatening you.

ARTIST. All right, what about begging me for mercy? You've not been down on your knees yet.

VICTIM. It wouldn't have any effect on you, would it?

ARTIST. You could try. (*The VICTIM slowly goes down on his knees before the ARTIST.*)

VICTIM. Have mercy.

ARTIST. Again.

VICTIM. Have mercy.

ARTIST. Again.

VICTIM. Mercy!

ARTIST. (*very cold*) I can't be involved.

VICTIM. (*after pause*) I've done wrong. I have done wrong.

ARTIST. What about going through the door?

VICTIM. It. . . . it's too late.

ARTIST. Not even a genuine death-bed repentance.

VICTIM. Why don't you kill me and get it over?

ARTIST. Is that the mercy you're begging me for?

VICTIM. If you're going to kill me, it would be a mercy to kill me quickly.

ARTIST. I am going to kill you. But it seems to me that you don't deserve a quick death. No, things are beginning to take shape nicely. The pattern's falling into place.

VICTIM. What are you going to do? (*He rises.*)

ARTIST. Something unexpected.

VICTIM. You've decided?

ARTIST. I think I know how you're going to die.

VICTIM. Get it over!

ARTIST. How are you feeling? You look weak. Are you beginning to feel ill?

VICTIM. Don't. . . . don't torture me. I . . . I didn't mean any harm.

ARTIST. The door?

VICTIM. No, no, I can't. I'm ready to die. I'm quite ready.

ARTIST. What courage! How long can you keep it up?

VICTIM. I'm afraid. I am afraid. But. . . . I'm ready.

ARTIST. I'm afraid. I am afraid. . . . that I'm not ready. Not yet. Soon, but not yet.

VICTIM. When?

ARTIST. Soon. In the near future.

VICTIM. How will you kill me?

ARTIST. In a very artistic way. A very fitting way. Worthy of you, and worthy of me.

VICTIM. (*trying to assert himself*) There. . . . there's a way I can foil you. I can ruin all your plans.

ARTIST. Suicide? You?

VICTIM. I can do it.

ARTIST. But you wanted more time, didn't you? More time, not less time! You'd have less if you did it yourself.

VICTIM. But I wouldn't suffer.

ARTIST. As you like. Which is it to be? Sleeping pills? Rope? Knife? Gun? (*He produces all these items from his pockets, and puts them on the table.*) There's a wide choice. Any preference? The pills are the least painful. If you just swallow this lot here, you'll simply go to sleep and never wake up. When you take them, of course, you'll know you're not going to wake up. That's the only painful bit. And the knife's messy and inclined to be slow. (*He sticks it in the table.*) The gun is the quickest of them all—if you aim straight. Anyway, I'll leave them here and you can think it over.

VICTIM. What do you mean. . . . you'll leave them?

ARTIST. You didn't see me come in, did you?

VICTIM. No.

ARTIST. Must have given you quite a surprise. Well, you'll be getting another surprise.

VICTIM. Do you mean you're not going to kill me?

ARTIST. Oh I am. Very soon. I'll be back almost before you've realised I've gone. (*He moves slowly towards the back right-hand corner.*)

VICTIM. How are you going to kill me?

ARTIST. It's all worked out.

VICTIM. Don't. . . . don't go!

ARTIST. You want me to stay? You want me to stay here with you?

VICTIM. I want . . . to know. . . .

ARTIST. Very soon. Take my word for it—very soon. I'll be with you again. . . . quicker than it would take you to open this door. (*He goes.*)

VICTIM. Wait! Wait! (*Slight pause*) You're there. I know you're there. How are you going to do it? (*Silence*) How? (*He stands behind his table, facing the audience.*) Go away! (*He sits down.*) You're bluffing. Well, you can't bluff me. You can keep your pills, your rope. (*He seizes a bundle of notes.*) You can keep your knife and your gun. (*He turns sharply to look at the corner. Silence.*) This is my home. And I've done no harm. (*Silence*) ONE, TWO, THREE, FOUR, FIVE, SIX. . . . SEVEN

. . . EIGHT . . . (*silence*) Are you there? (*Silence*) ARE YOU THERE? (*Silence: he looks sharply round at the corner again. All is still. He faces the front again.*) Are you there?

THE CURTAIN FALLS

THE END

The Wall

a play in one act

CHARACTERS

JOHN-JOHN (J.J.)
DOLORES (DOLL)
OLD MAN

SCENE: A wall
TIME: The present

THE WALL was first performed by the Theatergruppe der Universitat Konstanz, West Germany, on May 10th, 1972, directed by the author.

The Wall

The scene is a huge wall, which covers the entire back of the stage. Chalked on the wall are the words 'The Wall'. JOHN-JOHN enters from the left.

J-J. Heigh, doll, come an' look at this. (*DOLORES enters from the left.*) Look at that.

DOLL. Blimey. (*They study the wall in silence for a while.*) Big, innit?

J-J. Colossal.

DOLL. (*jerking her head at the words written on the wall*) Bloody silly.

J-J. (*reading*) "The Wall". Not exactly original.

DOLL. We can do better'n that.

J-J. I should hope so. Gotcher chalk?

DOLL. Yeah. (*She takes some chalk out of her bosom.*) What about you? (*He shows her the chalk in his hand.*)

J-J. You go first.

DOLL. All right. (*She approaches the wall decisively, raises the chalk, then waits.*)

J-J. Go on.

DOLL. I'm thinkin'.

J-J. What for?

DOLL. What to write, stupid.

J-J. Shouldn't be too difficult. With all that brickwork.

DOLL. I think we should rub that off first. Disturbs yer concentration.

J-J. All right. (*He takes a handkerchief from his pocket, and wipes off the words "The Wall".*) That any better? (*She stands back.*)

DOLL. Yeah.

J-J. Right.

DOLL. Right. (*She marches up to the wall again, and decisively writes the letter 'M'. Then she stops.*)

J-J. Whatcher stoppin' for?

DOLL. I'm thinkin'.

J-J. M. Mother.

DOLL. Marx.

J-J. Well go on then, write it.

DOLL. I don't know. What about Lenin an' all them? I mean, Lenin, you know, an' Trotsky an' Stalin an' whoever they all are. I mean . . . what about them?

J-J. Well write Marx, an' see where it leads you.

DOLL. I know where it'll lead me — to Lenin an' all that lot. That's why I've stopped.

J-J. At M.

DOLL. Yeah.

J-J. Write somethin' else then.

DOLL. Like what?

J-J. Muggins.

DOLL. What's that mean?

J-J. Doesn't have to mean anything, does it?

DOLL. It does. You might just as well leave 'The Wall' on it if you're not going to write sense.

J-J. All right, then. Moses.

DOLL. He was a Jew.

J-J. So what?

DOLL. Then you'd have to start going into details. Circumcision an' all that sort o' thing.

J-J. No bacon, except at business. Well, try Mozart.

DOLL. Who?

J-J. Mozart.

DOLL. What for?

J-J. To start us off. Mozart.

DOLL. Here, Johnnie, what d'you think's on the other side o' this wall?

J-J. On the other side o' this wall, I expect there's the other side o' the wall. Like this side, only the other way round.

DOLL. But I mean, where we're standin'.

J-J. Prob'ly a place for people to stand just like this one.

DOLL. Maybe somebody's over there now.

J-J. (*shouting*) Anybody over there? (*Silence*) Nobody.

DOLL. Maybe they're deaf.

J-J. Maybe. What you goin' to write?

DOLL. I dunno. I don't think it should start with M, though. Wipe it off, Johnnie. (*He wipes it off.*) That's better. You write somethin'. (*JOHN-JOHN writes 'Sex' on the wall.*)

J-J. How's that?

DOLL. Typical.

J-J. Looks all right.

DOLL. It's been done before.

J-J. So what?

DOLL. Well, it's been done before.

J-J. Course it's been done before! Doesn't make any difference. It still looks all right.

DOLL. It looks dirty.

J-J. Get away.

DOLL. It does. It's crude.

J-J. It's all right.

DOLL. Wipe it off.

J-J. I won't. (*He writes 'Sex' again, next to the first one.*)

DOLL. Oh blimey!

J-J. Can you think of anything better?

DOLL. Every bloody wall it's the same. One track, that's you. (*He writes 'M' on the wall.*)

J-J. (*bowing*) Madame?

DOLL. I'd sooner write nothing than filth.

J-J. I'm the opposite. I'd sooner write filth than anything.

DOLL. I got that message a long time ago.

J-J. Well, there's your M — let's have the rest.

DOLL. I think I'd prefer S. (*JOHN-JOHN wipes off the M and writes an S instead. He stands back for a moment, then returns and adds 'ex'.*)

J-J. Obvious.

DOLL. I was thinking of Shakespeare.

J-J. Like heck.

DOLL. I was.

J-J. You saw mine, and you were in complete agreement. We were on the same wave-length.

DOLL. Balls.

J-J. Exactly. (*DOLORES writes 'Shakespeare' on the wall.*)

DOLL. Shakespeare.

J-J. What's that meant to prove?

DOLL. I'm not tryin' to prove anything. I'm tryin' to get started.

J-J. Then how about this? (*He writes 'Genesis' on the wall.*) That's a start, isn't it?

DOLL. Very witty. (*He writes 'Adam' 'Eve' on the wall.*)

J-J. You know what that brings us to, don't you? (*He writes 'Sex' on the wall.*)

DOLL. Naturally.

J-J. In accordance with nature.

Doll. What are people goin' to think, when they see what we've written?

J-J. They'll think the bloke that wrote that must've been a genius.

Doll. They'll think he was a filthy bugger.

J-J. And they'll never know what vile language he had to put up with.

Doll. We ought to write somethin' clean.

J-J. Clean. (*He thinks for a moment, then writes 'Virgin' on the wall.*) How's that? No. No, there's somethin' missin'. (*He writes, next to it, 'deflowered'.*) That's more like it.

Doll. More like you. Anyone who sees this'd think there was only one thing that mattered.

J-J. Who's goin' to see it anyway?

Doll. We saw it.

J-J. Well we happened to come by.

Doll. Maybe somebody else will too. You never know.

J-J. Well let 'em come. I've got nothin' to hide.

Doll. You never had.

J-J. I'm not ashamed of what I'm writin'. There's a lot worse you could write than that.

Doll. Such as? (*In quick succession, JOHN-JOHN writes 'Old Age', 'Poverty', 'Illness', 'Loneliness', 'Death'.*)

J-J. You want me to go on?

Doll. No.

(*An OLD MAN hobbles on left.*)

Old Man. Excuse me. (*They are both startled.*)

J-J. Blimey.

Old Man. I wonder if you can help me.

J-J. We were . . . we were just writing on the wall.

Old Man. I'm looking for my little dog. I seem to have lost him.

J-J. Your dog?

Old Man. A little terrier.

Doll. What's 'is name?

Old Man. I. . . . I just call him dog. He usually answers when I call him, but he seems to have run away. You haven't seen him?

J-J. Haven't seen any dog round here. You, Doll?

Doll. No.

OLD MAN. Ah, I see . . . I see you've been writing on the wall.

J-J. Eh? Oh yes. (*Laughing*) Just a bit, you know. Nothing startling, like.

OLD MAN. I used to write on the wall, too.

J-J. Oh yes.

OLD MAN. Last time, do you know what I wrote?

J-J. No idea.

OLD MAN. I wrote the words 'The wall'. I couldn't think of anything else worth writing.

J-J. No. Well, we're just getting our hand in, you know.

OLD MAN. I don't see the words there any more. I suppose someone came along and rubbed them out.

J-J. Yes, I suppose so.

DOLL. What does your dog look like?

OLD MAN. He's just a terrier. Ordinary. Dog, that's his name.

DOLL. Well we haven't seen him, anyway. We'll let you know if we do.

OLD MAN. Very kind. (*He is reluctant to go, and continues to gaze at the wall.*) You seem very interested in sex.

J-J. Who, me? Oh, um well, you know. . . . um. . . . a bit of fun. It's just. . . . you know. . . . something to write.

DOLL. Your dog's certainly not been here, 'cos we'd 'ave seen 'im.

OLD MAN. Now who wrote 'Shakespeare'?

J-J. Bacon? Ha, ha. (*He looks from one to the other, but doesn't get any reaction, so stops grinning.*)

DOLL. I did. Why?

OLD MAN. Makes a change. I'm very fond of Shakespeare. Especially the Psalms. Most inspiring.

J-J. The Psalms?

OLD MAN. So uplifting. Let me have the chalk a minute, will you? (*He takes the chalk from JOHN-JOHN, and goes to the wall. He writes, next to JOHN-JOHN's list: "Why standest thou afar off?"*) Uplifting. Goodbye. (*He returns the chalk to JOHN-JOHN.*) So nice to have met you.

J-J. We'll let you know if we see your dog.

OLD MAN. Dog? Oh, yes, the dog. Thank you. (*He hobbles off right.*)

DOLL. Blimey, the Psalms by Shakespeare.

J-J. The Gospel according to St. Mark Antony. Anyway, he liked the sexy bit.

DOLL. He didn't. He was only being polite.

J-J. He was slobberin' over *your* tits.

Doll. Don't be filthy. (*JOHN-JOHN writes 'Tits' on the wall.*)

Doll. Do you think he really had lost a dog?

J-J. 'Spect so. Why should he lie to us?

Doll. Maybe he was embarrassed. Wanted something to talk about.

J-J. He looked the type who'd have a little dog. Looked the type who'd lose it, too.

Doll. I didn't like him very much.

J-J. Not our sort.

Doll. Not our generation. Frightening. (*JOHN-JOHN writes 'Dog' on the wall.*)

J-J. Dog. Perhaps it should have a small letter. Dog. (*He writes 'dog' on the wall.*)

Doll. Can't we write some poetry, or somethin'? Instead of odd bits an' pieces?

J-J. Like what?

Doll. I don't know. Poetry. There must be some poetry we could write.

J-J. Suggest something.

Doll. I can't write poetry.

J-J. Nor can I.

Doll. We should be able to think of something. . . . sort of. . . . joined together.

J-J. Siamese twins.

Doll. Oh you an' your bloody sense o' 'umour.

J-J. Well somethin' joined together like what? You're full o'bright ideas, but you never get down to details, do you? I mean, it's all destructive. What have you written so far? 'M' and 'Shakespeare'. Bloody inspired.

Doll. Maybe we should write somethin' political.

J-J. You started off with Marx, if I remember rightly—or leftly.

Doll. No, I mean a message.

J-J. Us, write a political message? What the hell have *we* got to say? Vote no. No vote.

Doll. Somethin' original.

J-J. Some hopes!

Doll. Well it's stupid just writin' odd words on the wall. They don't mean anythin'. (*JOHN-JOHN writes on the wall: "Politicians are all bloody selfish sods".*)

J-J. How's that?

DOLL. Not very rational, is it?

J-J. You write somethin' better, then. (*She thinks for a moment, then writes "Summertime".*) What's that supposed to mean?

DOLL. Summertime.

J-J. I know. What's it mean?

DOLL. (*shrugging her shoulders*) I don't know. It just came to me.

J-J. Genius. Why don't we try associations.

DOLL. All right. You start. (*He writes 'Sex'. She writes 'Love'. He writes 'Sex'.*) That won't lead us anywhere.

J-J. All right. Try again. (*He writes 'Money'. She writes 'Money'. He writes 'Money'.*)

DOLL. We're not gettin' anywhere.

J-J. Where d'you expect to get?

DOLL. Johnnie, can't we write somethin' worthwhile? Just for once?

J-J. What can *we* write, Doll? We're both a couple of ignorant sods, never 'ad a worthwhile thought in our lives.

DOLL. (*gesturing towards wall*) But I mean, look, there's all this.

J-J. Could do a big drawin'.

DOLL. It'd have to be good.

J-J. Then we needn't bother.

DOLL. We could try.

J-J. You do one that end, an' I'll do one this end.

DOLL. All right. (*They draw at opposite ends of the wall. JOHN-JOHN, very crudely, draws a naked woman. DOLORES, very crudely, draws a man and a woman holding hands.*)

J-J. (*when half-way through*) How's it goin'?

DOLL. All right. You?

J-J. Just gettin' to the interestin' bit. (*They finish together. Each stands back to look.*)

DOLL. Let's see yours.

J-J. All right. (*They cross over to look at each other's.*)

J-J.
DOLL. (*simultaneously*) Oh blimey, look at that.
I might have known.

J-J. (*to DOLORES*)
DOLL. (*to J-J*) You're crude.

OLD MAN. (*singing off-stage*)

Lacrymosa dies illa,
Qua resurget ex favilla
Judicandus canis reus.

(*They listen to the singing. The OLD MAN comes on, carrying
a newspaper. He stops singing when he sees JOHN-JOHN
and DOLORES.*)

OLD MAN. Oh, are you still here? I hadn't expected to find you
here. I'd expected you to be gone.

DOLL. We're still here.

OLD MAN. My dog—you remember?—it's confirmed in
today's newspaper, with all the war and the killing, you know.

J-J. Is he dead?

OLD MAN. Missing. It's been confirmed. A terrible blow.
After all these years. I had him since he was born—blind as a
kitten, but so sensitive! It's a terrible blow to lose one's com-
panion—especially at my age. There are so few of us about. I
rather depended on him.

J-J. Can't you get yourself another?

OLD MAN. Where? (*An anguished cry*) Where? Help me,
young man, help me! Where?

J-J. Get away from me!

OLD MAN. (*turning to DOLORES*) Help me! Won't you
help me?

DOLL. Get off! Leave us alone!

OLD MAN. I need help!

DOLL. Johnnie, get him off!

OLD MAN. Please!

J-J. Get away, you ole tramp. (*He pulls him away from DO-
LORES.*) Go on, get out of it.

OLD MAN. I appeal to you.

J-J. Get out.

(*A momentary tableau. JOHN-JOHN stands with hand raised,
DOLORES is shying away, and the OLD MAN has his
hands out in supplication. Then JOHN-JOHN slaps the
OLD MAN's face, and movement continues. The OLD
MAN clutches his cheek and turns away, JOHN-JOHN
manfully stands his ground, and DOLORES goes behind
him, for protection.*)

OLD MAN. (*directly to audience*) Why art thou so far from helping me? I cry in the daytime, but thou hearest not; and in the night season, and am not silent. I am poured out like water, and all my bones are out of joint: my heart is like wax; it is melted in the midst of my bowels. My strength is dried up like a potsherd: and my tongue cleaveth to my jaws; and thou hast brought me into the dust of death. Deliver my soul from the sword; my darling from the power of the dog. (*Pause*)

J-J. Get out. (*The OLD MAN slowly shuffles off.*) Silly ole bastard.

DOLL. Let's go home, Johnnie.

J-J. Completely buggered up the whole bloody day. We've stiil got all that lot to fill in.

DOLL. I don't feel like it now.

J-J. Course not. Nor do I.

DOLL. Let's go home.

(*They go off. There is a pause. At length the OLD MAN returns. He wipes the words and drawings off the wall, takes a piece of chalk from his pocket, and writes the words 'The Wall', precisely as they were at the start of the play. As he finishes, the curtain falls.*)

THE CURTAIN FALLS

THE END

Wendlebury Day

a one-man play

CHARACTER

Tom Wendlebury

Scene: A pool of light
Time: The present

WENDLEBURY DAY was first performed on the fringe of the Edinburgh Festival on August 22nd 1977.

The part of Tom Wendlebury was played by Lloyd Lamble.

The play was directed by Bill Alexander.

Wendlebury Day

TOM WENDLEBURY, aged 60, stands in a large pool of light.
The rest of the stage is bare and in shadows.

TOM. (*spoofing*) Tell me the truth, doctor. I can take anything, and I'd rather know than not know.

I'm afraid . . .

No fear. Pretend that . . . I'm a total stranger. Treat me with detachment.

It's as we'd feared. You can't have more than a few weeks. Oh God!

No, no, you must be strong. I'm a stranger, remember.

How can you take it like that?

Every man must face this sooner or later. I'm fortunate to know when and where.

You're so calm, so brave.

I'm just an ordinary man.

Tom Wendlebury, you're a saint.

No, I'm flesh and blood like you. All too clearly flesh and blood.

He was just sixty years old. A man who had done everything. Writer, sportsman, politician, philanthropist extraordinary. At his funeral there were astonishing scenes, as women flung themselves sobbing onto his coffin. The Royal Family were present, as were many heads of state. The Royal Philharmonic Orchestra played his Requiem, sung by those members of the Royal Choral Society that were able to control their grief. A national day of mourning has been declared. His birthday will henceforth be known as Wendlebury Day. (*Pause, he looks round.*) Anybody there? Bastards, leave a man to die on his own?

Stay with me, Ellen. Stay with me. The only love. The love of a lifetime. That bitch in France . . . forty if she was a day! Ça ne suffit pas! My God, she should have paid me. Oh, and the smell! V.D. The shame of it! Doctor, I . . . I must have caught it from a lavatory.

Oh yes?

Could it have been my fiancee? I'll break off the engagement at once. Christ, what a bloody thing to say. Must have laughed his pants wet.

Tu veux faire l'amour, chéri? Hiding her shadows in the shadows. Remember the old heart thumping, going up those stairs, looking up her skirt ahead, and wondering what the hell I was supposed to do. That's where it all went wrong. You're supposed to know. Right from the cradle. Eat Ootsie-Wootsies' Baby Foods and be a father at six months.

Couldn't you find a less commercial means of engendering? They're all at it—rabid monkeys, unzipping their bananas. Father, Finch, and the rest of them.

There's more to life than that, Finch, I can tell you. Much more to life than that! Dead at forty-one because you didn't know there was more. But it takes a great man to see it—to capture it. And greatness stands alone. Because only the great man can keep pace, can bear the brightness of the vision. The darkness of the vision. The sadness of the vision. This strange, melancholy sadness of the poet, pervading all he does, all he says. Il pleure dans mon coeur . . .

Christ, what a bloody weed! Stand up and fight like a man! Mr. Wendlebury, this sensational victory. World Heavyweight Champion at the age of sixty . . . how did you do it?

It's a matter of being able to tap the potential resources. There's infinite strength, as in the atom, if it can be harnessed.

You knocked him out with just one punch.

Yes. Of course, if the fight had gone on, he would certainly have beaten me.

What are your plans now, Mr. Wendlebury?

I've proved my point, and so I shall retire from boxing. Undefeated Heavyweight Champion of the World. Muhammed Wendlebury. One shouldn't attach too much importance to these things. (*He 'spars' for a moment, then stops with a huff and a puff.*)

Ah well.

Anybody there?

Bastards.

When the house was pulled down, they found a skeleton in one of the attics. The man had been dead for at least ten years. No-one had ever thought of looking in there. One of the neighbours said: "I did sometimes wonder if 'e was all right, but I didn't like to interfere." Did it not occur to you, madam, that as ten years had passed without your setting eyes on him, something might be wrong?

"Well, 'e always did keep 'isself to 'isself." When you have been dead for ten years, madam, it's difficult to do otherwise.

Hello, St. Peter.

Hello, Mr. Wendlebury. Had a good death?

Most impressive. Took me breath away.

So you're Tom Wendlebury. May I tell you how much I admire your work. Thank you, Mr. Shakespeare. You're not untalented yourself.

Tom Wendlebury — writer, composer, heavyweight champion of the world . . . ah, but which world? Tom Wendlebury. Who the hell is Tom Wendlebury? A man of action? A man of thought? The Great Lover . . . Oh yes, there was this girl in Paris . . . girl . . . well, a mature woman . . . I never knew her name — Sandra Soofipa or something like that. Beautiful woman. Took me back to her flat after just a moment's acquaintance. Gave me everything. And when I left her, she was crying. Shouting, to be more precise. I was lucky to get away with my life and other . . . properties. But I can honestly say that I went off with more than when I'd . . . got on. Three months it took to cure.

Then there was Helena. The girl I should have married. She wasn't beautiful — no, by no stretch of the imagination could anyone have called Helena beautiful. Ugly, yes, but not beautiful. I loved her. For twelve years we went out together. It was another of those whirlwind affairs. And then, on the stroke of make-your-mind-up time, she threw herself away on George Belfitt — a dull, smelly nonentity. Was George Belfit sexually attracted to her? That's another of the miracles. For every hippopotamus there's a hippopotama to set the hippopotabells a-ringing. I'd marry her today if she were here. To get away from these accursed silences! (*Silence*) Is anybody there?

Did God feel like this before he created man?

Your Royal Highness, my lords, fellows of the Royal Society, imagine a machine that can register an unlimited amount of data, process them and use them constructively at will. Imagine that this machine could look after itself, and adapt itself to changing circumstances. And imagine also that it could — astonishingly — reproduce itself. Would you not then marvel at the genius of the inventor? Would you not then say his must be the greatest intelligence known to us? Your Royal Highness, my lords, fellow . . . fellows, such a machine does exist. You are looking at it. Why then do you not marvel at the intelligence of the inventor? Why do you impute the most miraculous, most complicated machine ever created to the forces of chance, when you would laugh to scorn anyone who even suggested that the very chairs you are sitting on could have been made by anything other than an intelligent, conscious craftsman? Evolution? Can you believe that matter could suddenly reproduce itself, and then suddenly by chance that same matter sprouted organs that needed to combine with other suddenly sprouting organs in order to reproduce—and sprouted them in perfect working order first go, because otherwise there would have been no reproduction? And can you believe that suddenly there came into being a perfect working eye, and a perfect working ear, nose, tongue, fin, wing—all suddenly leaping from nowhere into perfect functional existence? The evolutionists will say: "But it wasn't sudden." They'll say it all took millions of years. But imagine an eye that couldn't see, reproducing itself until it could—a wing that couldn't fly, an ear that couldn't hear. Imagine a penis that couldn't quite achieve anything, but just hung around till it could enter another lump of matter that also took centuries to sort itself out. And both of them clinging to the old-fashioned do-it-yourself technique till the new method got itself right. You see, my lords, a mutation *is* sudden, and therein lies the soft centre of the theory of evolution: the unbelievable miracles cloaked by the word 'mutation'. You would scoff if I told you Chance built a television set, and yet you believe implicitly that Chance built the brain which created television. You marvel at the blind faith of the martyrs, yet you believe in miracles far greater than any they knew of.

Science. The blind, painting landscapes.

No-one listens—only you, perhaps, committed to silence.

I can't go on. I can go on. I don't know if I can go on.

I can't invent anything real, you see, doctor, that's the trouble. Nothing to confirm that *I'm* real.

Of course you're real. At the moment. Yesterday may have been a dream and tomorrow may be an illusion, but at the moment you're real. Professor of Philosophy, Thomas Wendlebury, thinker . . . (*He raises his arm in pose of Rodin's Thinker, and sniffs his armpit.*) . . . Stinker.

If I'd married Ellen, I'd have had a clean shirt every day, regular meals, company.

Mr. and Mrs. Thomas Wendlebury. Day after day, night after night. The ugly Ellen, snuggling. . . . I'd never be able to do it. Not with her. No. So I showed her. Just as I showed Finch. Bastard, leave those girls alone! Finch was a married man. My father was a married man. Finch, father, father, Finch.

How she suffered, knowing what he was doing. Night after night. Of course she killed him. What else could she have done?

Take a grip, Wendlebury, that way madness lies.

I could go out. See people living without me. Buy something to get myself acknowledged. But I'd only have to come back and start all over again. Help me, doctor.

You don't need help. You're in total command of yourself. It's sheer apathy that's your enemy. Too lazy to exploit the infinite potential. Use every gift God has given you—use it now, before the book closes. Tom Wendlebury, this is your life.

Born on a mountain top in Tennessee. . . . your mother was a virgin, humble, lower class origins. Do you recognize this voice?

I'll fuck 'em all. Bring 'em here, an' I'll fuck 'em, every one of 'em.

Yes, your dear father. Robert Wendlebury.

Hello, father.

Hello, son.

How are you?

Shagged out.

Now Robert Wendlebury, tell us your earliest memories of your son Tom.

Memories of Tom. My memories of Tom are very clear. Who's Tom?

When you left school, Mr. Wendlebury, you obtained employment with the firm of Peabody and Peabody, manufacturers of fancy goods. Do you remember this voice?

Tom, I have plans for expansion. I'm thinking particularly of Western Europe. You seem a bright lad. I'm sending you to France for a year. Familiarize yourself with the French market.

Ho, ho, the French market! You remember France, Tom? Just over the water there. You had a good time in France. Do you recognize this voice? Tu veux fair l'amour, chéri? C'est la première fois? Voilà! Bravo! T'as fini? Qu'est-ce que c'est? Ça ne suffit pas, hein! Ça ne suffit pas! Yes, your first love, scooped up from the holy shadows of the Madeleine.

I *did* make love to her, pox and all. And she was alive.

Don Juandlebury, to what do you attribute your colossal success with women?

I don't know. They just. . . . come to me.

How could God conceive of male and female? God created man in his own image, in the image of God created he him; male and female created he them.

Why?

An ingenious antidote to isolation—making companionship the key to survival. But how could he conceive it?

Because, my dear fellow, he's very very clever. That much is due, whatever the final judgment.

The final judgment. You can't judge me independently of my father and mother.

The horror. All that blood. Couldn't you have poisoned him instead? Oh yes, doctor, I saw it all. I was eight years old. Eight.

No, I won't tell you what happened. Silence, that's the only wisdom. Like God's.

I created you as an entertainment — a diversion from the long winter night of eternity. The fish in the one-way glass bowl. Your best hope for optimism is to recall that humour can only be produced by a sense of humour. Beyond that, there's little cause for optimism. Even I begin to find it all . . . appalling.

Then why don't you change it?

Maybe he doesn't find it appalling. (*Pause*) That would be the ultimate horror.

Well, I may be trapped, and I may be helpless, but you can't stop me thinking, unless you kill me — and then you lose me. Dictators kill, but the victims are the heroes.

Dead hero. Big deal.

So, Thomas Vendlebury, you defy me, ha? You refuse to bend ze knee. Very well, ve heff ways off dealink viz pipple like you. Bring ze burnink irons. Aaaargh! Pull out hiss fingerniles. Aaaargh! Now try pickink your nose, you English fool!

They stretched him on the rack, burned him, tickled him, starved him, parched him, mutilated him. . . . but Thomas stood firm, until his tormentors, broken in spirit, fell to their knees in admiration, begging his forgiveness. And he forgave them, saying: "They knew not what they did." But you do know. You have a lot to answer for — and no-one to answer to.

So might is right, and the law of the jungle's your law. So why punish her, since she was stronger than him? She was right to kill him.

Was she?

No, Mummy, no, Mummy, stop it, stop it! All that blood. Don't take her away. Don't take Mummy away!

Hello, darling. Come. Come. Now, are they looking after you? You're not afraid are you? Tell me, are they looking after you?

He never saw her again.

Tell me, Tom, what do you remember of the years that followed? The institution. . . .

Grey. Unrelieved grey. One set of grey to the next. Walls, and more walls.

And the years after you returned from France? What happened to them?

Can't remember. Ellen, yes, but. . . . nothing else. Nothing at all. Nothing before Finch.

Come now, there's thirty years before Finch. What happened in those thirty years?

I don't remember.

No-one can have a blank thirty years long.

I remember Ellen.

All right, tell me about Ellen.

We met. . . . where was it? Monte Carlo, the gaming tables? Or was it Tahiti, 'neath the palm trees?

Where did you meet?

Vine Street Methodist Church. I'd fallen from heaven. She was five foot three, plump, wore glasses and a flowery dress. It was the beginning of the greatest love story since. . . . Annan and Chi-Chi. Sunday after Sunday we hymned our God and drifted ever closer, pew by pew. Until at last, one Christmas Day, we were side by side, and she dropped her handkerchief. A flowery handkerchief, I recall, that was neatly ironed and virginally unsnotted. I picked it up and returned it to her, and our fingers touched, with the momentary shock of physical contact. She smiled. I smiled back. We were as one. We lay down in the aisle, tearing off each other's clothes, and as the ninety-year-old verger rattled his collection-box above us, we reached our first orgasm. The choir sang hymn number 42: "O God, Thou bottomless abyss". The vicar sprinkled holy water over us, and under us, and blessed our union. God remained in heaven, for all was right with the world.

Three months later, she told me her name. Ellen. I introduced myself to her as Muhammed Ben Muhammed, writer, composer, adored missionary, and heavyweight champion of the world. She was overwhelmed. We were married at St. Paul's Cathedral, by his majesty the Pope, accompanied by his three sons George, Alexander and Giveup. It was the wedding of the century. She wore a flowered handkerchief, embroidered with her new initials. I wore an illuminated manuscript of hymn number 42. We spent our honeymoon at the Vatican, leaving after six months of hectic fornication, during which we saw each other only at press conferences. Our first child was born just two weeks later—a premature hermaphrodite called Edward, who was blessed with a full set of teeth that resulted in a painful amputation for my wife. Our second child, Nancy, was a strapping boy of some six feet. One on each leg. It was a blissfully happy marriage. We understood each other even without speaking. Indeed speech became superfluous. In fact, impossible. She came from an extraordinary family, I remember. Her father was an accountant for a modelling agency of no fixed address. Her mother was a policeman. Neither of them came to our wedding, partly because it was not their concern, and partly because they were dead. I didn't hold it against them.

It's a remarkable story.

I've led a remarkable life. From the age of about 25 up until the age of about 60, I remember nothing except my tragic passion for Ellen.

What happened to her?

We lost touch. Simply lost touch.

This George Belfitt, who took her from you. How could a genius like yourself lose to a complete non-entity of that ilk?

I didn't lose her. I gave her to him, in the subtlest way imaginable. I wore her. . . . down. I wore her. . . . away. I never, in twelve years, touched her.

You were 25 when you met?

Yes.

And 37 when she left you?

Time flies when you're having fun.

You remember nothing else?

Nothing officer. I'm suffering from a coitus interruptus of the memory.

Mr. Wendlebury, why did you kill her? I warn you that anything you say may be taken down as evidence and used in the News of the World.

I had to officer, it's the beast in me.

And the others?

An irresistible force.

Look at him, the monster. Imagine, all those women he killed.

Bluebeard, Jack the Ripper, Christie, Tom Wendlebury. And the greatest of them all was Tom Wendlebury.

Won't you come in, my dear, just for a minute? See my little collection of. . . . rare prints from the Karma Sutra? And a little cup of coffee. That's right. Now you sit there. Good. Just right. Don't turn round. Where's the axe? What a nice white neck you have. Swish.

Twenty headless bodies immured behind the flowery wallpaper. And pride of place to dear Ellen, who left me.

He's a monster.

But a fascinating monster.

Is it a joke? (*Pause*)

Now, gentleman, if God made man in his own image, it must follow that God is also the image of man. This surely tells us all we need to know about his nature, which is inevitably reflected in the nature of our own man-made world. He is the supreme embodiment of the virtues and the vices he has created. Unfortunately, it also means that he will be unpredictable, prejudiced in his judgments, arbitrary in his decisions. He is all that is good, kind and generous. There's grounds for hope. He is all that is dark and pitiless. Grounds for despair. Given the duality of God, so perfectly mirrored in ourselves — his image — and the world he and we have created, there remains nothing but the question of motive. Simple. How else could he enjoy the entertainment, if it were not in terms he could relate to himself?

But Sir Thomas, this is heresy. They'll burn you.

I stand for truth.

Thomas, my love, renounce what you have said, for my sake!

No. The truth is paramount.

The inquisitors pronounced their savage sentence. There were gasps of horror in the court.

"You may burn my body," he told them calmly, "but my spirit will live on to prove you wrong."

Executioner, light the fire.

Sir Thomas, oi 'as to do it. Oi can't help it. Say you forgive me, Sir Thomas.

Thou shalt be with me in paradise.

The relics of St. Thomas are to be found in Wendlebury Cathedral.

Strange that I've never been summoned to the palace. The prophet, as always, ignored in his own country.

I'm honoured to meet you, Sir Thomas.

Your Majesty is too kind.

Such a rich life.

I've had my moments.

Have you ever kissed a Queen?

Mmmmmmmmmm! My little crown jewel.

This is so wrong.

And yet. . . . so right.

The Scandal that Rocked a Nation.

Thomas Wendlebury first met the Queen when she knighted him after his epic single-handed voyage round the world. The moment she laid the sword upon his shoulder and felt the current crackling back up the blade, she knew he was the man of her destiny. Arise, Sir Thomas, she said, and meet me round the back of the refreshment tent in half an hour. Thirty-five minutes later, he went to meet her. She was disguised as a Coca-Cola hoarding, but he recognised her immediately by the lion and the unicorn stamped on her left buttock.

I love you, she said.

It cannot be, said Thomas. Remember your position.

I'll do it in any position, she said. Only say that you love me.

But you're a Queen, said Thomas.

I am also, she said, a woman.

Not here, said Thomas.

Where? Oh where?

My catamaran.

This is no time for worrying about your pets.

No, it cannot be. My duty calls me elsewhere, to the pounding waves, and the rising, setting suns. Farewell, and God bless England.

So saying, he stepped aboard the boat that had already weathered so many rougher storms, and sailed slowly away towards the setting sun.

A rich life indeed.

Hello? (*Silence*)

Maybe if I had some work to do, it'd be easier. Keep the mind off the mind.

I worked for forty years, and it didn't help me. Order forms, catalogues, letters, tea, Finch. Finch! Finch at every step, Finch round every corner, Finch in the doorway, Finch in the chair.

Tell us about Finch, Mr. Wendlebury.

Finch?

Albert Finch.

I don't know any Finch.

Come now, you worked in the same office for ten years. He's your immediate superior. Albert Finch.

Ah yes, of course. Albert Finch.

Where were you on the night of the murder?

The murder?

Where were you?

But I didn't know he'd been murdered.

Didn't you?

Why no, this is a terrible shock.

When did you last see him?

I saw him. . . . oh, Friday, at the office.

You didn't see him after you left the office?

No, no.

There are three witnesses who can testify that you and he drank together at the Dirty Dog.

The Dirty Dog?

The Dirty Dog.

Albert Finch and I?

You and Albert Finch.

Three witnesses. Ah yes, of course. This is so confusing. Friday, of course. We often went to the Dirty Dog on Fridays.

What happened when you left the Dirty Dog?

When we left the Dirty Dog? When Albert and I departed from the Dirty Dog? Why, he went his way. . . . and I went my way. Tell me, officer, oh tell me, how did poor Albert meet his . . . . untimely end?

We were hoping you could tell us that, Mr. Wendlebury.

I? I? Me? But I know nothing, officer. As you could see, I was completely taken aback by the news. Shocked, Incredulous. Dear Albert dead? What about his poor wife? All his children, born in and out of wedlock? This is the most appalling tragedy. Oh, officer, he was my best friend. My only friend. How can I go on if Albert is dead? Albert dead? I don't believe it. Officer, tell me it isn't true. It isn't true, is it, officer? It's some kind of macabre joke. Can it be April 1st today? No, alas, alas! Albert gone for ever. Oh, the pity of it, Iago. Who, oh who could have wanted to chop off Albert's head with an axe that was made in Sheffield?

One moment, Mr. Wendlebury. How did you know that Albert Finch's head was chopped off with an axe that was made in Sheffield?

How did I know? Why you. . . . you said so yourself.

I did not.

It was in all the newspapers.

Not that it was made in Sheffield.

It. . . . it's a known fact.

Known to no-one except me. . . . and the murderer.

Then you. . . . are the murderer? Save me, save me!

No, Mr. Wendlebury. You are. You've been very clever, Mr. Wendlebury, but not clever enough.

Don't count your chickens yet, officer. I have one or two eggs left up my sleeve. I shall plead insanity.

You're crazy.

No I'm not. It was a crime of passion. The jury will have to set me free.

You admit, then, that you killed him.

Certainly not. I've never heard of Albert Finch. Albert Finch — who's he? In this country, officer, a man is innocent until proved guilty. I shall conduct my own defence. You see, gentlemen of the jury, I am not guilty. Therefore I am innocent.

Brilliant. An astonishing defence. That a layman should have such a total grasp of the intricacies of the law! Mr. Wendlebury, we have no alternative but to set you free.

Scenes of jubilation at Old Bailey as Tom Wendlebury wins case. There were unparalleled scenes of jubilation today as 60-year-old Tom Wendlebury was acquitted of the murder of Albert Finch. The handsome Wendlebury was cheered by large crowds as he left the Centre Court after one of the greatest men's singles finals in history. Police formed a cordon to hold off the many screaming women that fought merely to touch their hero. Tom Wendlebury himself remained calm and unruffled after his triumph. "It was nothing," he said. "My opponent, Albert Finch, simply lost his head."

Such are the turning-points of human history.

What man has the right to judge me, anyway? They talk as if the law were superhuman. But men write it, and men enforce it, so who the hell do they think they are? Judges, Kings, Queens, Politicians — they're not so high and mighty with their trousers round their ankles.

Sic transit gloria mundi. Gloria's not well, but she'll be passing through next washday.

So, George Belfitt, you speak Latin? Ah no, of course not. You teach it instead. Forgive me for my little joke, George. . . . may I call you George? Humour's one of the few pleasures left to me. As Ellen will tell you, I've always hidden my pain beneath a smile. The worm beneath the marble. But believe me, I am quite sincere in wishing you every happiness and joy in the years ahead.

No, I'm not bitter. Should I have invited you if I'd felt un-happy at your. . . . forthcoming union with Ellen? She was a fine girl. What? Oh no, a mere slip of the tongue. Is, is! Won't you have a drink? Just a little drink?

How easy it all is, when it's properly planned. But how the heart thumps till one's grown used to it.

Her scarf, her scarf in the bathroom. Yes indeed, she *was*

here. You take it, George. Swish. One day I shall write my memoirs, and give the world the secret of my success. Success! Aaaaargh! I repeat: aaaargh! The Scream by Thomas Wendlebury. Novel of the century. Won't you send me somebody? (*Silence*) You won't. Fair enough. You created your diversions, so I must create mine. Create, or disintegrate. How fertile am I? Pretty fertile — I've kept going for sixty years. I can think back, think forward; I can invent and interpret; I can ask, answer, and ask again; I can romanticize, fictionalize, rhapsodize; I can accuse, defend, and judge. I'll defend myself by accusing you. The trial of Thomas Wendlebury. Prosecuting Counsel, the Lord God Almighty. Counsel for the Defence, the great man himself.

I claim that all my weaknesses sprang from a fault in the original design. If a house falls down, do you blame the occupant or the architect?

Heroic, Thomas, but pointless. The rules are mine. Even King Canute would have drowned if he hadn't moved.

But even if I did move, Lord, I'd have no guarantee you wouldn't drown me.

True, Thomas, very true.

So why bother to move?

Weigh up the chances, Thomas.

I'd have a better chance if I cringed?

If one little boy put his hand in yours and said, "I'll go where-ever you go," and the other little boy blew you a raspberry and kicked you up the backside, which of them would you take to the sweetshop with you?

You're a persuasive talker, Lord.

I have my moments, Thomas.

So I should start cringing. On creaking knees I ask you please forgive all my iniquities. Words without thoughts never to heaven go. Perhaps it would be easier, Lord, if *you* were to repent.

You're forgetting again, Thomas: I make the rules.

Which brings us back to where we started. The geometry of philosophy — every figure a circle, every reality a globe. No beginning, no end — only the unbreakable roundness. Nothing certain, nothing defined — total . . . indeterminacy.

You are the supreme artist, Lord.

Thank you, Thomas.

If you're still there.

Who knows?

Oh God, help me!

Thomas, help yourself.

I shall go mad.

But that's what you want, isn't it? That's what you're really after with all of us. Watching the toy soldiers blow themselves up. Well, you won't get that satisfaction—not out of me. Because I've got a weapon to fight it off with.

Keep laughing, that's the secret. Take the whole thing as a joke. Ha, ha, some joke! Keep laughing. There's nothing under the sun that isn't funny. Sex, perversion, God, religion, murder, death . . .

There was this lunatic. Every day he would stand in front of the mirror and shout: "I can see God, I can see God!" Day after day in front of the mirror: "I can see God, I can see God!" And this gradually got on the other patients' nerves, until one day he'd just stood in front of the mirror when one of the patients leapt up, pulled the mirror off the wall, and flung it down on the floor. The mirror was smashed to pieces. And the lunatic looked down at the reflections in the thousands of shattered fragments at his feet, and the shock drove him sane.

I don't find that funny. No, that's not funny. Nothing's funny. There's a darker side to all things, and all days turn to night. All nights turn to day. And then it's night again. You see, doctor, I'm losing my sense of humour. Once I was always quick to see the joke—the funny side. If someone fell on a banana skin and broke his leg, I'd always be the first to split my sides. These women that kept coming to me like flies to a spider and telling me they loved me—I laughed and laughed and laughed . . . for thirty years. Even Finch . . . ultimately I saw the joke. Or made him into a joke. But now . . . I can only think of the horror. It isn't funny any more. Doctor, give me something to relieve me, will you? Please.

What's wrong with you?

What's wrong with me? Ah! Didn't you say I was going to die? Dying. My God! There must be an escape. Nothing in this universe is single-sided. The deeds are done. Are they recorded? Who interprets them? Just you?

I'm not dying. This is absurd. Who said I was dying? Beyond the normal ebbing of the time. I'm alive, ready, willing, able to go on.

To go on with what?

A cause—that's what's missing. An incentive, to make us feel it's worth the effort.

Woman saves herself from flames by leaping from 12th floor. Breaks neck on pavement below.

Falling tree just misses lucky old man. Lucky old man dies of shock.

It's not true. I'm making excuses. The present is real, regardless of what the future does to it. The truth is that I'm not a hero, not a saint, not a genius, not even heavyweight champioin of the world. What *am* I?

In a single word?

In a single definition. Who is Thomas Wendlebury?

Through whose eyes?

Your own. (*Pause*)

Philosopher.

Ho. Ho ho. A fine alibi.

A madman. No, I won't accept that. I'm conscious — madmen aren't conscious.

Tell us the truth.

The truth, the truth. How can I remember it? After all that's happened, and not happened.

You do remember.

No.

Give us a factual account of your existence so far. Just facts.

I was born sixty years ago. (*Pause*)

Go on.

I'm alone now and ill.

Your life!

No.

Everything that happened. The meat of it.

Fantasy. Illusion.

Your mother and father. Just the facts. Who they were, how they died.

Everyone knows the facts.

Ellen. Who she was. How she died. George Belfitt. Who he was. How he died. Who everyone was. How everyone died. The facts. Let them out, into the air, so we can look at them, assess them, assess you.

I was born sixty years ago. My mother was kind, affectionate, gentle. My father used to joggle me on his knee. I was their only child and they worshipped me. I was school captain, and later gained first-class honours in Modern Languages at Cambridge. On coming down, I entered the firm of Peabody and Peabody, beginnng as a clerk and finishing as managing director. In my forties I was elected Councillor, then Alderman, and finally Lord Mayor. At the age of thirty, I had married Helena Belfitt, who bore me three sons who are now my fellow directors. Helena and I are still in love and are extremely happy. There are no clouds on the horizon. Life is simple.

I was born sixty years ago. My father was a miner, my mother used to take in washing. I was the seventh of twelve children. We were very poor and lived in a three-roomed dwelling in the North of England. My father died when I was eight, my mother when I was twelve, and my two elder brothers soon afterwards. My elder sisters were imprisoned for prostitution, and I was put in care. When I was fifteen, I became an errand boy at Peabody and Peabody's. I fell in love with Ellen, but my first duty was to my brothers and sisters. For twelve years I struggled to earn enough money to ensure their survival. I lost Ellen to a teacher named George Belfitt — their marriage was desperately unhappy. I rose through the firm of Peabody and Peabody, ultimately achieving the managing directorship. My brothers and sisters are now all happily married. I alone am without a family of my own. Sometimes I reflect sadly on what might have been, but in my heart I am at peace, because I have done right.

My life story should be filmed.

Which life story?

I was born sixty years ago. My father was constantly unfaithful to my mother, who murdered him when I was eight years old. My mother went insane, and died some years later in a lunatic asylum. I was put in care. When I was fifteen, I became an errand boy at the firm of Peabody and Peabody, where I worked diligently, cleverly concealing from everyone the fact that I was a homicidal maniac. My first victim was a girl called Ellen, who had jilted me. For good measure, I also murdered the man she intended to marry. I then carried out a series of murders that completely baffled the police, my victims being girls whom I would drug, rape, and then decapitate. I made steady progress at the firm of Peabody and Peabody, and should have been given the managership of the export department. The job was given instead to a newcomer who reminded me of my father. I killed him, but was unluckily detected, arrested, tried, and found insane. My effigy is to be found in the Chamber of Horrors at Madame Tussauds's. I have been interviewed by psychologists, criminologists, and newspaper reporters, and my name is a household word.

The truth? Let us face up to the truth.

I was born sixty years ago. In that time I have learnt nothing, enjoyed nothing, achieved nothing. I've tried to understand the nature of life, the nature of the world, the nature of God, but the search has brought no pleasure, no certainty. I have conducted it alone, and have suffered alone. This I regard as typical of the human condition. I am a world famous philosopher, and yet my fame brings me no more satisfaction than my fruitless search for the truth. I am ready for death, for in death I now see the only hope for advancement along the paths of knowledge. I see reason to fear God, and little reason to love him. I am afraid to face him, because I believe I am in his image. It is possible that I have misunderstood everything, as my brain is puny, my reasoning preconditioned, my perception three-dimensional. I am the fool God made me. I am unhappy.

I was born sixty years ago. I have devoted my life to finding out why. And in the search I have uncovered miracle after miracle, equating myself with every living creature, and finding in every living creature the unending, unstinting ingenuity of God. For every decision I have taken, I have been aware of a hundred untaken decisions; for every question, a hundred answers; for every verse, a hundred melodies. And I have found that for every winter there is a spring, for every death a birth, for every dusk a dawn. I know that each mystery is insoluble, and this is a source of wonderment, not of despair. I do not wish to die, because I do not wish to leave the incomparable richness of this world. I am the fool God made me. I am happy.

LIGHT OUT

THE END

The Fourth Prisoner

a play in two scenes

CHARACTERS

Sean
Jack
Lamb
Three Figures

Scene: A prison cell
Time: The present

The Fourth Prisoner

SCENE ONE

As the curtain rises we see a prison cell, round in shape, grey in colour. High up in the wall at the back there are two barred windows, below and between them is a small ventilator grille, and directly below the grille is a door. On each side of the cell is a double-decker bunk. SEAN—middle-aged or beyond— is on the top right bunk, smoking. JACK, younger, is on the left.

SEAN. (*traces of Irish*) Grey walls, grey floor, grey ceiling, grey bloody everythin'. Even the smoke comes out grey, though I'm givin' it the purest oxygen I got.

JACK. You must 'ave filthy nitrogen.

SEAN. Ah sure, that'll be it. Diluted. (*Pause*) You know somethin' I've often wondered? Why is it that when you breathe in, you take in nought point nought four per cent of carbon dioxide, an' when you breathe out the little bastards 'ave made themselves into four point five?

JACK. I wouldn't worry about it if I were you.

SEAN. Now at that rate, we're not goin' to get by for very long before we run out of the bloomin' stuff altogether. An' then what do we do?

JACK. Write to your local M.P.

SEAN. Do you think there's such a thing as a carbon dioxide transfusion?

JACK. Yes, mate, they give yer a gallon of carbonic acid every night before yer go to bed. Then when yer get up in the mornin' they give yer a special asbestos bowl to piss in. (*Pause*)

SEAN. There's another thing. You breathe in twenty point nine six per cent of oxygen, but when you breathe out, do you know what's left? Sixteen point five. So every time you breathes in, there's nearly four and a half per cent of oxygen gets left behind. In a year or two I reckon I'll be floatin'.

JACK. Yer won't float very far in 'ere.

SEAN. All the same, I've noticed I've a tendency to run to fat—

87

an' I'm not so sure that the fat is all fat. I've a sneakin' feelin'
that I'm gettin' blown up inside, like a balloon.

JACK. Yer'd better stop breathin', then, 'adn't yer?

SEAN. Ah, that'd be one solution.

JACK. Where'd yer get all the gen from?

SEAN. (*pulling a book out from under his pillow*) Human
Physiology. Filthy book. Very interestin'.

JACK. Any pictures?

SEAN. Well, there's the author on the back cover, if that's any
use to you.

JACK. Man or woman?

SEAN. Kind of . . . half way.

JACK. What's inside?

SEAN. All gone. There's others just as frustrated as yourself.

JACK. I'd like ter see 'em. 'Specially the women.

SEAN. Ah, the ragin' o' the blood. 'Tis a terrible thing to be
young.

JACK. It is when yer stuck in 'ere.

SEAN. You'll be in for a long while yet.

JACK. As long as you?

SEAN. If they go accordin' to the book. God help us all.

JACK. This new bloke don't seem too 'appy.

SEAN. Ah, he'll fret himself to death. I seen his type before.
He'll bash his head against the wall till his brain falls out. 'Tis no
good bein' here if you've not got the patience.

JACK. There ain't no choice, is there?

SEAN. All the more reason for bein' patient.

JACK. I wouldn't mind if there was some bloody birds around,
but stuck in 'ere all yer life. . . .

(*The door opens, and LAMB, early twenties, is pushed in. The
door closes again.*)

LAMB. Damn them!

JACK. Taken all the partic'lars, 'ave they?

LAMB. They treat you like animals. Who do they think they are?

JACK. You'll get used to it.

LAMB. I'm not staying long enough to get used to it.

JACK. Yer a lifer, ain't yer?

LAMB. A lifer! A lifer! I'm getting out, that's all. (*He bangs
his fist against the door.*) Let me out of here! Open this door!
Open up!

(*Chorus of voices from outside: "Shut Up! Belt Up!" etc.*)

SEAN. 'Tis no use carryin' on like that, Lamb, we're all in the same position. (*LAMB goes to the bunk below SEAN, and lies down on it. SEAN, leaning over the edge:*) Would you like to be readin' a book, all about the human body?

LAMB. Keep it. (*Pause*)

SEAN. You know, Jack, there's one other thing that bothers me. You breathes in seventy-nine per cent of nitrogen — and when you breathes out, you know what the figure is?

JACK. Go on.

SEAN. Seventy-nine. The same. Now that means that seventy-nine per cent of the energy you spends breathin' is a complete waste of time. It strikes me that there's some mighty lousy plannin' been goin' on somewhere. If you could cut out the nitrogen breathin' you'd probably live seventy-nine per cent longer.

JACK. Yer a genius.

SEAN. If only there was a way of cuttin' out this nitrogen altogether. A nitrogen filter or somethin'.

LAMB. How long are you going to keep this up?

SEAN. (*leaning over again*) Keep what up?

LAMB. This stupid conversation.

SEAN. Is it botherin' you?

LAMB. I want some peace and quiet.

SEAN. Ah you'll be gettin' plenty of that. There's time enough for silence when we've finished talking.

LAMB. Well finish now, will you?

JACK. You was saying, Sean, that this seventy-nine per cent goes in, and seventy-nine comes out, wasn't you?

SEAN. That is what I was sayin', Jack.

JACK. Well what makes you so certain that it's the *same* seventy-nine goes out as what goes in?

LAMB. Stop it, will you?

JACK. Sean and me's 'havin' a conversation, do you mind?

LAMB. (*standing up*) I do mind.

JACK. Then put yer fingers in yer ears.

LAMB. (*crossing the cell to JACK's bunk*) Now look here. . . . (*In one movement JACK jumps down to the floor. He towers over LAMB.*)

JACK. What? What is it, Mr. Lamb?

LAMB. I don't like your attitude.

JACK. I don't like *your* attitude! So it's mutual, ain't it? You don't like my attitude, an' I don't like your attitude, so we ought ter get on fine. (*LAMB turns away, and goes back to his bunk.*)

SEAN. Ah Lamb, 'tis no use takin' on like that. Resignation, that's the great virtue. Is it not, Jack? Resignation, and the willingness to make big pleasures out o' the little pleasures. There's some that's put in solitary confinement, and they're worse off than we are.

LAMB. Worse off! Worse off! Who could be worse off than me?

SEAN. Ah, self pity is a terrible thing. Is it not a terrible thing, Jack, to pity yourself?

JACK. Terrible.

SEAN. Make the best of it, Lamb. Set your mind to thinkin' of other things.

LAMB. Like nitrogen!

SEAN. Ah, he has a sense o' humour. Thank the Lord for a sign o' human warmth. Sure, you'll have us in fits before we pass away. Will he not Jack?

JACK. (*gloomily*) We'll be in 'ysterics.

SEAN. There's two things that keeps us alive — conversation, an' a sense o' humour. D' you hear me, Lamb — two things. . . .

LAMB. Leave me alone, can't you?

SEAN. 'Tis a film star you should have been. A bloody film star. (*Silence*)

JACK. Say somethin', Sean, will yer?

SEAN. Say somethin'? Now, what shall I say, then? Is there a subject you'd like to broach?

JACK. Anythin', mate, anythin' at all, except birds.

SEAN. You're havin' your monthly, are you?

JACK. Gettin' more like weekly.

SEAN. Well, I could read to you, but the on'y book I got is this human physiology. . . .

JACK. No, just talk, anythin'll do.

SEAN. Talk. Well . . . er . . . talk.

JACK. Come on, Sean.

SEAN. Ah, he's put me right off me stroke. I'll sing to you instead. (*Deep rough bass:*)

"If you ever go across the sea to Ireland,
  If you ever go across the sea to Ireland,
  If you ever go across the sea to Ireland,
  You can say you've been across the Irish Sea."
How's that then?

JACK. Fine. Keep going.

SEAN. That's the end.

JACK. Sing another one, then.

SEAN. Well, um . . .

"A hot-headed feller from Wrotham
Lost his trousers and didn't know who'd got 'em.
Though his head was so hot,
He died like a shot,
From a terrible cold in the. . . ."

Ah, 'tis a terrible vulgar song, though.

JACK. Can't yer think o' somethin' that'll go on a bit longer?

SEAN. Well, not entertainin'.

(*LAMB jumps up, rushes to the door, and thumps on it again with his fists.*)

LAMB. Let me out! Let me out! Let me out! (*Again the Chorus from outside; LAMB, gradually subsiding:*) Let me out! Let me out! Let me out! (*SEAN eases himself down from his bunk, and goes across to LAMB.*)

SEAN. Take it easy, Lamb, take it easy. There's no point in carryin' on like that. They'll not let you out.

LAMB. They've got to let me out. They've got to.

SEAN. They let you out when it's time for you to be let out — you can't hurry them.

LAMB. I shouldn't be in here.

JACK. Yer can say that again.

LAMB. They've got no right to put me in here.

SEAN. Ah, who can say that it's right or wrong?

LAMB. I haven't done anything. You don't understand — I'm an innocent man. I've done nothing. I've committed no crime, I . . . I've defrauded no-one, harmed no-one, deceived no-one. I'm an innocent man.

SEAN. 'Tis a terrible dull life you must have led.

LAMB. They've got to let me out.

SEAN. Now listen, listen. You're in here, whether you like it or not. An' as companions of the order, you've got Randy Jack over there, an' Smilin' Sean over here, again whether you like it or not. Now the choice lies between fightin' us, or joinin' us. I'm invitin' you to join us.

LAMB. I just want to go.

SEAN. Sure you do. Are you with us, or against us?

LAMB. Look . . . I . . . I don't think you've quite understood . . . I . . . I'm not like you — I'm innocent.

SEAN. I can see it. You're a lovely young feller.

LAMB. I've done nothing wrong. They've made a mistake. I shouldn't be here.

SEAN. Son, the point isn't that you shouldn't be here. The point is that you *are* here. And there's your Uncle Sean an' your cousin Jack to keep you company. Me with me lovely stories an' conversation, an' Jack with his lovely thoughts about women. All set for an eternity of bliss. For or against?

LAMB. I've got nothing against you . . .

SEAN. Then that's all right. That's the basis for a perfect friendship. Now let me go an' lie down. I'm exhausted. (*He returns to his bunk.*)

LAMB. I . . . I'm sorry if I made a fool of myself.

SEAN. Think nothin' of it. If you didn't, someone else would. Now we can get on with the business of livin'. Are you all right, Jack?

JACK. Fine. 'Avin' a whale of a time. Sun shinin', beach beautiful, birds smashin', wish you was 'ere, see yer soon, luv Jack.

SEAN. That's the spirit. (*LAMB goes over to JACK.*)

LAMB. I'm sorry about that little scene.

JACK. 'Sall right, mate. We all 'ave our moments.

LAMB. (*after slight pause*) What are you in here for? (*JACK sits up and looks hard at him.*)

JACK. We don't ask that kind o' question 'ere, mate! We keep quiet! We don't think about it! (*He grabs LAMB by the collar and jerks him close.*) D'you understand? Eh?

LAMB. (*scared*) Yes, I understand.

SEAN. Take it easy, Jack, he didn't know it.

JACK. I don't like that sort of question! (*He lets LAMB go.*) That's all.

LAMB. I didn't mean to offend you.

SEAN. Come an' lie on your soft iron bedspread, Lamb. Conserve your energy. You'll soon get used to things. (*LAMB obeys.*) That's better. Now we're all at rest. Conservin' our energy. Isn't that a lovely feelin'. All the energy pilin' up inside you, just like the little stock-pile of oxygen that's blowin' me belly out into a bubble.

JACK. An' what the bleedin' 'ell are yer gointer do with the energy?

SEAN. What am I goin' to do with it? I'm goin' to rush round the world, collectin' up all the carbon dioxide that the people are breathin' out from the precious little lot they was born with, an' I'll set up a carbon dioxide bank—the first carbon dioxide bank in the world. Isn't that a beautiful thought? (*LAMB is quietly crying.*)

JACK. 'E's cryin'. (*SEAN leans over to have a look.*)

SEAN. Ah, this young feller's goin' to be the death of me. (*He heaves himself down from his bunk again.*) Come on now, son, snap out of it — you can't sleep on a wet blanket.

LAMB. I want to go!

SEAN. Sure, sure, all in good time!

LAMB. Why should this happen to me? I've done nothing.

SEAN. All right, now listen to me, son, listen to me. You think you're the only one, don't you? Eh, is that right?

LAMB. I didn't say that.

SEAN. But you're thinkin' it. Well you're not the only one. Jack over there doesn't know what he's done. I don't know what I've done. But we're here. For some reason that no-one has ever told us, and no-one's ever going to tell us, we're here, an' the choice is between belly-achin' till your guts fall out, or makin' the best of a bloody awful job. So we don't ask questions, we don't try an' beat the livin' daylights out o' the door, we don't piss in our pants, an' we kid ourselves as best we can that it's all for the best, an' life's a grand experience. Jack's got a nasty temper an' a morbid turn o' mind, but him an' me gets on all right cos we got used to each other, so cut out the April showers and see if you can't turn on a bit o' sunshine — just to make things a bit easier for us, eh?

LAMB. I didn't know you . . . were in the same position.

SEAN. Nobody ever does. It comes with experience.

LAMB. Do you think we'll ever be let out?

SEAN. Sure we'll be let out! There's a limit to everythin'.

LAMB. And what do you do to pass the time?

SEAN. That's the great problem. How to get through the days and the weeks and the months and the long bloody years. But we manage. Eh, Jack? We manage, don't we?

JACK. We survive, if that's what yer mean by managin'.

LAMB. Have you two always been alone till now?

SEAN. Oh no. They never leave us alone for very long. There's all kinds have slept in your bed, boyo, all kinds. Only none of them ever stayed long. Old Jack smells somethin' terrible when he's sweatin'. I whispered it in his ear once, you know. "B.O.!" That's why the girls never liked him. Couldn't stand his armpits.

LAMB. What about the other bed?

SEAN. Ah no, we've never had nobody there. There's usually three of us, but we've never had a fourth. It's a good thing. He farts in his sleep. You know, Jack, it's a thing I've wondered about before. Why they never give us a fourth. They've made all the provisions for him, but they never send him.

JACK. Per'aps they've left it vacant fer us — alternative accommodation. If we feel like a move — change o' scenery, then we can shift 'ouse to flat four.

SEAN. That's a lovely idea. Come an' spend your holidays in Bum View. Enjoy the fresh sea breezes. But 'tis a terrible waste of a good bed. D'you think we should advertise it?

JACK. Chuck a note out the window, eh? Wanted, attractive girl to fill vacant position. Permanent post.

SEAN. With beautiful prospects.

JACK. Shorthand not required.

SEAN. Long legs preferable.

JACK. Experience an advantage.

SEAN. The trouble with havin' a woman though is that you can't relax. You can't even have a g   ⁴ swear.

JACK. I'd sooner 'ave a woman an' cut out swearin'.

SEAN. Ah no, Jack, a sense o' proportion, boy. A man's got to be able to relax in his own home.

JACK. A fine bloody relaxation all this is.

LAMB. If nobody's ever been in the fourth bed, why are the blankets and things rumpled up?

SEAN. That's true. You've got a pair of eyes on you, haven't you? Well there was a fellow there once — name of Johnnie somethin' or other.

LAMB. What happened to him?

SEAN. He killed himself. Fine lookin' chap he was, with a beard.

JACK. (*leaping down from his bunk*) Come on, I'll take yer both on. (*He stands in a wrestling pose.*)

SEAN. Oh give us a break, will you, Jack? I'm worn out through lack o' carbon dioxide.

JACK. I gotter keep in trim. I'll take yer both on.

SEAN. All right. Come on, Lamb.

LAMB. What for?

SEAN. It's his trainin'. (*JACK takes off his shirt, and for the first time we see what a superb physical specimen he is. SEAN strips down to his vest and trousers, and LAMB does the same.*)

LAMB. What are we supposed to do? (*JACK has held up both his arms, wrists turned outwards.*)

SEAN. You take his right, I'll take his left. We're supposed to try an' push him back. (*They take up positions.*) Are you ready? Shove. (*There is a tremendous amount of pushing and groaning*

—especially from SEAN, but slowly JACK pushes them both back until they are up against the bunks. Then he lets them go.) Phew! You're not a man, you're a bloody elephant.

JACK. Yer out o' condition, that's what's wrong with you.

SEAN. 'Tis all the oxygen inside o' me—makes me light as a feather. Anyways, I wasn't gettin' a great deal o' help, was I?

LAMB. I'm not a sporting type.

SEAN. Ah, more the intellectual, eh? Have you never learned how to take care of yourself?

LAMB. No.

SEAN. Did you hear that, Jack—the young lad's never learned to take care of himself. Come here. (*He motions him to the centre of the stage.*) Now take a swing at me jaw, me poor, brittle, unguarded old jaw. Go on, hit it. (*LAMB pokes out his fist and SEAN, with a surprisingly rapid movement, grasps his wrist and flicks him off balance. LAMB falls with a crash.*) If you've not got the body, you have to have the brain. You see, Jack an' me has a mutual respect. I'm scared stiff o' his body, an' he's terrified o' my brain. 'Tis the ideal marriage. (*From the floor LAMB dives at SEAN's legs, and brings him down very heavily. He grabs SEAN's throat, and is evidently trying to throttle him. SEAN with a great effort, throws him off. LAMB hurls himself at the door, again hammering at it with his fists, until gradually he sinks to his knees, and remains crumpled and dejected on the floor. SEAN gets up fingering his neck, and spits on the floor. Then he heaves himself onto his bunk. JACK, who has watched all this impassively, is sitting on the edge of his bunk by now. There is a long silence.*)

JACK. Nearly 'ad yer chips there, then.

SEAN. He's took me whole bloody store of oxygen.

JACK. It's one way o' goin', innit?

SEAN. I'll go when it's me turn.

JACK. What's the difference—now or later?

SEAN. (*annoyed*) There's every difference! If there was an ounce of brain hidden in that ton o' muscle, you'd be shiverin' in your boots.

JACK. It's bloody stupid ter think about it like you do. No guts.

SEAN. Guts? Guts? Since when was you so gutsy? You can't even stand five minutes o' blessed silence.

JACK. That ain't me guts, it's me 'ormones.

SEAN. Scared o' them, scared o' yourself, whichever it is, I'm the one that has to fight the silence.

JACK. Yer not tryin' ter kid me yer like silence, are yer?

SEAN. I don't like it.

JACK. Well then.

SEAN. Well then what?

JACK. Don't make out yer talkin' fer my sake.

SEAN. I'd not do nothin' for your sake. I'd do nothin' for no-one — just like yourself. But if you're talkin' o' guts, Jack Harris, don't try to de-gut me. I've thought it all out and I've faced up to it. You could never see beyond half way down your body.

JACK. At least I ain't ashamed ter look at me body.

SEAN. An' you're dead scared to look anywhere else.

JACK. I'm scared o' nothin'.

SEAN. You're scared of every bloody minute o' the day.

JACK. Me? Who's talkin'?

SEAN. I'm talkin' — as it's always me who's talkin'. Keepin' off the mental dry rot, savin' you while I'm savin' meself.

JACK. Savin' from what? Go on, answer. Savin' from what?

SEAN. From silence. Despair. Suicide. You'd be another John-nie if it wan't for me.

JACK. Johnnie never killed hisself, an' you know it.

SEAN. Johnnie killed himself. There's no arguin' about it. . . .

JACK. You killed 'im like you'd kill the rest of us if you 'ad the chance.

SEAN. You're crazy.

JACK. I'm not crazy. I know what went on. I know what. . . .

(*There is a metallic click, and a VOICE comes out through a loud-speaker.*)

VOICE. Jack Harris. Cell Three. Jack Harris.

SEAN. Christ!

JACK. What's it mean, Sean?

SEAN. They're comin' for you.

JACK. For me?

SEAN. It's all up, Jack. You're a gonner. (*JACK leaps from his bed, and rushes to the door, pushing LAMB aside.*)

JACK. They won't get me that easy.

SEAN. Come over here, son. Come right out o' the way. Good luck, Jack. (*LAMB moves away from the door.*) Right over here, son. It don't do to get too close. (*LAMB, watching JACK all the time, backs away to his bunk. JACK puts his hands against the door, in the same position as when he fought SEAN and LAMB. Suddenly we see him take the strain. Then there is a tremendous duel between himself and the door. SEAN, quietly:*) Go on, Jack, push 'em back. Push the bleedin' bastards back. (*JACK begins to slip.*) Fight 'em boy, fight 'em.

(*For a moment JACK holds his ground, but then again he slips, and slowly the door is forced open. JACK goes down to his knees, but is still pushed backwards, until finally he lets go and the door swings back against the wall. Two figures, covered from top to toe in black, emerge from the doorway, place themselves on either side of JACK, and drag him out. The door closes. There is a long silence.*)

SEAN. In the prime of life. They take a handsome, healthy hunk of a boy like that, an' leave a fat ole bastard like me, an' a miserable little moaner like you. There's no justice.

LAMB. What will they do to him?

SEAN. Serve him up as an Irish Stew. How the hell should I know? Maybe they'll give him a harem to work through. Except that them fellers that come for 'im didn't look none too sociable. If they're all like that, Jack'll have a job tellin' the difference. He put up a good fight, though, did he not? All his muscles bulgin' out like a gorilla. He was in good trim, was Jack. Fat lot o' good it did him.

LAMB. How can you take it so damn lightly?

SEAN. Cos I'm in here, an' he's out there, that's how. Makes the blankets feel twice as warm. Yes, poor ole Jack. I never thought I'd outlast him — but there it is, let that be a lesson to the world: the brain outlasts the muscle. When you think about it, he'd have kept 'em off just as long be runnin' away as he did be tryin' to push 'em. An' I'm thinkin' it's a bit humiliatin' when a feller gives it all he's got an' can't make no impression. If he'd ha' run away, at least he could have said he'd kept somethin' in reserve. Poor divil looked as if he hadn't an ounce o' carbon dioxide left in his body. Anyways, Lamb, you can take over his bed, now. The upper berth is always healthier than the lower. More oxygen an' not so much stinkin' nitrogen. Requiescat in pace.

LAMB. Sean, I'm scared.

SEAN. *You're* scared! Me pants is ringin' wet, an' *you're* scared! Can you not hear me dentures playin' The Flight o' the Bumble Bee? Jack an' me was buddies. I knew him before you was thought of, an' I'm grievin' for him, but I'm grievin' with a smile on me face, because it's me what's grievin' for him, an' not the other way round. Every coffin has a velvet linin'. Now go an' make yourself at home up there in that bed o' sin.

LAMB. Will they change the sheets?

SEAN. Ah sure, son, sure, just pull the bell-rope an' ask for the chambermaid. You change the bloody sheets yourself in this establishment. An' if there's any dirty shirts or pants up there you'd better hold your breath till you can get rid of 'em.

LAMB. I don't see how you can be so calm.

SEAN. Experience, me boy, experience. I've learned me lessons in the classroom of life, death was me teacher, and wisdom me reward. (*LAMB begins his task of removing JACK's things, and replacing them with his own.*) Mind you, it's not goin' to be so easy now he's gone — unless you manage to develop into a decent listener. Do you think you've finished with bangin' on the door an' massagin' me Adam's Apple, or is that goin' to be a regular routine, like?

LAMB. I'm sorry. I didn't mean to do what I did.

SEAN. That's all right. As long as I can close both me eyes when I go to sleep. Bung them things under the fourth bed. Smells don't go through iron. You know, that's somethin' that's always puzzled me. There's sound waves an' light waves, but nobody ever talks of smell waves. Has that ever occurred to you, Lamb? If a skunk could travel faster than the speed of smell do you think he'd knock himself out? Smell waves. If you could trap 'em on a kind o' smelly tape recorder, Chanel would be out o' business in a week. There's undiscovered territories in the air, you know. It's not all nitrogen an' oxygen an' carbon dioxide. An' I'll tell you another thing — a real mystery. Are you listenin'?

LAMB. Yes.

SEAN. Well, it's this. When you breathe in, you take in nought point nought four per cent carbon dioxide. Right? When you breathe out, there's four point five carbon dioxide. Now assumin' that everybody's breathin', how does it happen that by the time you take your next breath — an' everybody else takes his next breath — that four point five per cent has vanished away and is replaced on the spot by another lump of air with nought point nought four? You follow that problem? If I was to breathe out, an' then at top speed swallow the air I'd just breathed out, who the hell's goin' to tell me I'm missin' four point four six of the carbon dioxide I just got rid of, an' by pure chance I'm grabbin' hold of just that quantity of oxygen to take its place? There's somethin' wrong somewhere.

LAMB. Sean, tell me about Johnnie.

SEAN. Johnnie? What's Johnnie got to do with my breathin'?

LAMB. I want to know about him.

SEAN. There's nothin' to tell. He had a beard, an' he killed himself.

LAMB. Jack said you killed him.

SEAN. I never killed him! That's just stupid talk. I was no more responsible for killin' him than his father an' mother was, bringin' him into the world.

LAMB. Why did he kill himself?

SEAN. At a guess, because he was fed up with livin'. That's the usual reason, isn't it? I'd prefer to change the subject, if you don't mind.

LAMB. What was he like as a person?

SEAN. He was two-legged, two-eyed, two-eared, like everybody else.

LAMB. But his character?

SEAN. What's so important to you about Johnnie?

LAMB. I want to know about him. (*By now LAMB has finished the transfer.*)

SEAN. All right. Put the light out, an' I'll tell you about him. (*LAMB turns off the light, and goes to his new bunk. A dim light continues to glow.*) Once upon a time, in the depths o' the deep dark forest, there lived a wicked witch named Grizzle-Guts. . . .

LAMB. Sean, I want to know about Johnnie.

SEAN. Johnnie. Well Johnnie was a clever one. Johnnie knew all the answers. Johnnie knew why we were here, an' he even knew why he was here, an' Johnnie was never scared o' bein' left here alone or o' bein' taken away out there. Johnnie slept at night, an' never woke up sweatin'. Johnnie could explain the past, comfort you in the present, an' give you somethin' to hope for in the future, as if the whole bloody lot somehow had a meanin'.

LAMB. And how did he die?

SEAN. How the hell should I know?

LAMB. You said he killed himself.

SEAN. That's what he did.

LAMB. How did he kill himself? Why did he? (*Long pause*)

SEAN. Do you not get the impression that this room's gettin' overcrowded wi' second-hand carbon dioxide?

LAMB. Did you kill him? Did you kill him, Sean?

SEAN. Nobody killed him.

LAMB. Then how did he die?

SEAN. 'Tis a mystery. Like every bloody death is a mystery. One moment you're inhaling the blessed oxygen an' spittin' out the lousy carbon dioxide, an' the next moment them black bastards come an' pull you away on out of it. Only they never come for him.

LAMB. Then how, Sean? What happened?

SEAN. He disappeared. An' that's the last question I'm goin' to answer. The Press Conference is over, an' Prime Minister Sean Murphy is off for a short vacation on the banks of the Maclethe river. Just put the Bournvita by the side o' me bed, cover me with a Candlewick, an' I'll bid you a fond goodnight.

LAMB. Sean, tell me about him. (*In answer, SEAN lets out a loud snore.*) Sean. (*There is a long silence. LAMB suddenly sits up in bed.*) Who is it? (*Complete silence except for SEAN's heavy breathing*) Sean? Oh damn you! What am I going to do? What am I going to do? (*There is a very soft "SH" sound, and a shadowy figure climbs out of the fourth bed and stands upright.*) Johnnie? Is it you, Johnnie? (*Very gently the figure pushes LAMB back, again making this soothing "SH" sound. We see him stroke LAMB's brow.*) What's going to happen to me? I'm scared, Johnnie.

FIGURE. (*whispering*) Sleep. Sh. Sleep.

THE CURTAIN FALLS

END OF ACT ONE

SCENE TWO

The following morning. The light is now full, but both men are still asleep.

LAMB. (*in his sleep*) Johnnie. Johnnie. Don't go. Don't go. (*There are stirrings from SEAN's bed. LAMB continues to mumble to Johnnie in his sleep. There is a great yawn from SEAN, who sits up, with some difficulty, screws up his eyes, and smacks his lips.*)

SEAN. Ah, so, I still haven't got to Heaven.

LAMB. Johnnie. Help me, Johnnie.

SEAN. (*looking around*) Who's he talkin' to?

LAMB. Johnnie.

SEAN. Oi, Lamb!

LAMB. Don't go! Don't go!

SEAN. Lamb!

LAMB. Help me!

SEAN. (*at the top of his voice*) LAMB! (*LAMB wakes with a start.*)

LAMB. Mm? What? What is it?

SEAN. Thank the Lord! I thought I'd gone dumb! You was talking in your sleep!

LAMB. Was I? (*He looks round the cell.*) Where's Johnnie?

SEAN. There's nobody here but us chickens. You was dreamin'.

LAMB. No. Johnnie's here. He was with me last night. When you were asleep.

SEAN. Oh. Oh, I see. Johnnie was here. An' you talked with him. That's lovely. That must 'ave been lovely for the two of yous.

LAMB. He *was* here, Sean.

SEAN. It was bad enough when ole Jack was there flexing his muscles an' his hormones, but them troubles was nothin' compared with you an' your do-it-yourself television.

LAMB. He was. . . .

SEAN. Son, Johnnie is dead, an' there's no ghosts where I live, an' I live here, do you understand?

LAMB. He was here, Sean. He spoke to me, he touched me. . . . (*SEAN heaves himself out of bed.*)

SEAN. The proof of the absence is in the absence. (*He whips the covers off the bunk beneath his own.*) Not in there. (*With considerable effort he gets down on his knees, and looks beneath the bunk.*) Two thousand years of dust an' not a sign o' Johnnie. (*He crosses to LAMB's bunk.*) Now then, Johnnie, you can come out of hidin'. . . . (*He whips the covers off bed number four.*) Your ole pal Sean is pinin' after you. Ah, the cunnin' divil, he's hid himself in the hot water bottle. All right, Johnnie, I know you're hidin' under the bed. There's no escapin' eagle-eyes Sean Murphy. Ha! (*He again goes down on his knees to search beneath the bunk.*) Dust to dust, an' ole Jack's sweaty shirt. Well he's not there either, little Lambkins, so if you haven't got him in bed with you, then he's not in here.

LAMB. He was here last night.

SEAN. Sure he was. He's here right now, aren't you, Johnnie? Ah 'tis good to see you, lad. You're not lookin' as well as you did when you was alive, but dyin' does make a difference to a feller's looks, wouldn't you say?

LAMB. Sean, he spoke with me, and he touched me! I'm not lying!

SEAN. Did I say you was lyin'? Son, there's not a man comes into the place that doesn't see Johnnie an' hear him. But it isn't Johnnie they see or hear. It's themselves. If I'd told you there was a feller name o' Michael died in that bed, then it'd ha' been Michael you'd have chatted with last night.

LAMB. I know he was here, and I know it wasn't my imagination.

SEAN. Well what makes you sure it was Johnnie? Why couldn't it ha' been poor ole Jack, sneakin' back for his underpants? Eh? How do you know it wasn't Jack?

LAMB. I just know.

SEAN. Ah, there's none so talkative as them that will not hear. If you're sure, you're sure. But next time he comes, ask him to bring a pint o' whisky with him, will you?

LAMB. He comforted me.

SEAN. So he did bring the whisky, did he?

LAMB. (*jumping down from his bed*) Perhaps he'll come again tonight.

SEAN. That's the spirit. Build up a future for yourself. Well now, a bright new day has dawned, bringin' with it the infinite variety of possibilities as to what we can do with ourselves. So what the hell are we going to do with ourselves?

LAMB. (*definitely more cheerful than before*) Do you think they'll send a replacement for Jack?

SEAN. A replacement for Jack? Sooner or later I suppose they will. There's usually three of us. But Jack an' me was buddies, you see—him an' me'd been together for a long while, so maybe they're changin' the system.

LAMB. Do they often change the system?

SEAN. Not in my memory. But what's one life-time?

LAMB. How long was Johnnie here?

SEAN. You're not startin' that bloody game again, are you? If it's questions about Johnnie you're goin' to be firin' at me all day, then I'll go back to sleep. Let's talk about the livin' for a change.

LAMB. Who?

SEAN. Well we can either talk about cheerful, lovable, everybody's darlin' Sean Murphy; or we can talk about you.

LAMB. All right. You talk, and I'll listen.

SEAN. It's always the same. Leave it to Sean, let him do all the hard thinkin', an' the rest of us'll sit on our behinds. Why don't you make a contribution to the general happiness of mankind? Go on, see if you can make *me* laugh.

LAMB. Why do you have to laugh?

SEAN. All right, then, make me cry if it gives you any pleasure. But do somethin' positive!

LAMB. Why do you always have to be doing something? Can't you relax?

SEAN. Questions, questions, nothin' but bloody questions! Life with you is like applying for a job twenty-four hours a day! Can you not give the interrogative a rest an' have a go at the affirmative?

LAMB. What do you want me to do?

SEAN. Anything! Anything at all.

LAMB. Well, why don't we tidy up in here?

SEAN. Affirmative, son, please.

LAMB. All right. Let's tidy up in here.

SEAN. That's a lovely idea. What an excitin', humorous occupation. Housework! All me life I've been searchin' for the occupation that would give me the greatest satisfaction, fillin' in the long an' painful hours with joy an' pleasure, an' at last the answer has come. (*Puts on woman's walk and voice*) Will you make the beds, sister, or shall I? (*LAMB has already begun picking up the sheets, etc., and now makes his own bed.*)

LAMB. You make yours, and I'll make mine.

SEAN. I got a better idea. You make yours, an' you make mine.

LAMB. I'll do my side, and you do your side.

SEAN. Ah, you're a bloody communist. (*He picks up the bedclothes from his side, and throws them on the top bunk.*) Finished. Now what do we do?

LAMB. I'm going to make Johnnie's bed.

SEAN. All right, all right. So long as you don't ask me no more questions about him, it's all right. Make Johnnie's bed for him, an' he'll kiss you goodnight like he was your own mother. (*LAMB finishes his own bed, and starts on Johnnie's. SEAN watches him for a moment, looking a little puzzled.*) Son, what did Johnnie say to you last night?

LAMB. Nothing much.

SEAN. What?

LAMB. He just. . . . told me everything would be all right.

SEAN. Is it that that's cheered you up today?

LAMB. Yes, it is.

SEAN. Supposin' I was to tell you that everythin' was not goin' to be all right. (*LAMB looks at him.*) Who would you believe?

LAMB. (*after pause*) Johnnie.

SEAN. Now why would that be, I wonder? Ole Sean, that's seen men comin' an' goin' like flies, that's got a lifetime's experience holdin' up the roof, that's standin' here as tangible as yourself, an' you take the word of a shadow.

LAMB. Johnnie knows, and you don't.

SEAN. Johnnie never knew a blind thing!

LAMB. He knows it all.

SEAN. Nothin'! How the hell would Johnnie know! You saw what happened to Jack, didn't you? Well I've seen it a thousand times — an' Johnnie took himself off before the others could get him, that's all there is to it!

LAMB. That isn't all! Sean, I know what happened to Johnnie.

SEAN. Oh he told you that too, did he?

LAMB. Yes, he told me! Everything. And he. . . .

SEAN. I don't want to hear it!

LAMB. . . . didn't kill. . . .

SEAN. (*shouting him down*) I don't want to hear it! You can talk till you're blue in the tongue, but I'll never believe you, not a word. Johnnie killed himself, an' there's no more to be said. Now find us a more entertaining subject, or indulge in a bit o' silence.

LAMB. You must have had a rotten life, Sean.

SEAN. Well I've had a life, an' that's more than some can say. An' who's goin' to judge whether or not it's been rotten?

LAMB. You know it yourself.

SEAN. I know no such thing! Ask all the dead men that's lived in here with me, ask them what they feel about Sean Murphy. Ask them who's filled in the bloody long silences for them an' who's given 'em a laugh to take the place o' the fear. What have you ever done for your fellow sufferers? I give them a moment. How long did you give them?

LAMB. How long did you give Johnnie?

SEAN. I give Johnnie what he wanted! I give him what he wanted! An' if he tells you otherwise, he's lyin'. Like all the martyrs an' all the saints — they forgive you for doin' what they asked you to do. (*Hauling himself up to his bunk*) Lamb, you've worn me out. Me voice an' me brain is pulverised. I don't know if I'm keepin' in the nitrogen or the oxygen. I'd shut up if it weren't for

the fact that you'd start talkin'. Askin' damn stupid questions.
Like: what was the colour o' Johnnie's eyes? Was his teeth white
or yeller? Did his bowels work regular? Isn't that what you'd be
doin', Lamb?

LAMB. No, I won't ask any more questions.

SEAN. There's a good lad. Don't mind me when I gets irritated,
it never lasts for longer than permanent. Rotten though I am,
I've got a heart o'gold. (*Silence*) Have you finished your housework?

LAMB. All that's worth doing.

SEAN. So what's next on the agenda?

LAMB. Meditation, I suppose.

SEAN. Ah, there's no fun in that. You know, I never realized
how much I used to enjoy fightin' wi' Jack. I used to think I was
doin' *him* a favour. Would you not be likin' a fight?

LAMB. No, I told you, I'm not the sporting kind.

SEAN. All the same, that wasn't a bad effort to throttle me yesterday. With a bit o' practice you might make it. How about it?

LAMB. No thanks.

SEAN. Well what are you goin' to do all day?

LAMB. What are *you* going to do?

SEAN. What I do depends on what you're willin' to do. If
you're not willin' to do nothin', then there's nothin' that I can do.
'Cept talk, I suppose.

LAMB. What about exploring?

SEAN. Exploring? Did you say 'exploring'?

LAMB. Yes.

SEAN. Exploring what?

LAMB. We could look out of the window for a start.

SEAN. Are you plannin' on growin'?

LAMB. You can lift me.

SEAN. There's nothin' to see out there. It'll only make you
more miserable bein' shut in here.

LAMB. I'd like to look all the same.

SEAN. An' you think I'm goin' to carry you?

LAMB. I'm not heavy.

SEAN. Now if you was to carry me, it might be a proposition,
but if you think I'm goin' to use up the few remainin' ounces
o' strength left in me body beautiful just so you can take a peep
beyond them bars, you can think again.

LAMB. If you'll lift me, I'll lift you.

SEAN. Are you serious?

LAMB. I'll try.

SEAN. All right, then. (*He climbs down from his bunk.*) I'll take you on. (*He places himself below the right hand window, spits on his hands and puffs out his chest.*) Now then. How do we go about it? Ah we should have had Jack here. He'd have picked the both of us up, one in each hand. If I was to bend down, could you stand on me back? (*He goes down on all fours.*) Come on. Er, shoes off first. Me feelin's is delicate. (*LAMB stands on SEAN's back, and remains a good three feet below the window.*) Can you see all right?

LAMB. About as well as you can. If you could stand up I might be able to see. (*LAMB perches near SEAN's shoulders.*) See if you can stand up.

SEAN. How can I stand up with you weighing me down? You'll have to get off. (*LAMB gets off. SEAN stands up.*) Ah, that's better. (*Looking straight at LAMB*) Do you have a better view now?

LAMB. I'll only be able to see if I'm standing on your shoulders.

SEAN. An' how do you propose to get up there?

LAMB. If you clasp your hands together, I'll put my foot in, and then step up onto your shoulders.

SEAN. An' supposin' me arms drop off?

LAMB. I'll risk it.

SEAN. It's not you I'm thinkin' about, it's me.

LAMB. Come on, let's try. (*SEAN clasps his hands together, just below waist height. LAMB puts his left foot in, then steps quickly up onto SEAN's shoulders, and grasps the bars of the window.*)

SEAN. Ouf!

LAMB. I'm up!

SEAN. An' you're through to me arm-pits already. What do you see?

LAMB. Sky. Blue sky.

SEAN. Try lookin' downwards.

LAMB. I don't know, it's sheer.

SEAN. Well look frontwards then. An' wash your feet next time.

LAMB. Just sky. (*SEAN suddenly ducks and steps away, leaving LAMB suspended hanging on to the bars.*) Oh!

SEAN. Ha! Now then, let's have a look at you.

LAMB. Sean! Sean, come back!

SEAN. You're a lovely sight, Lamby boy. I'd say you looked more like a monkey than a lamb. See if you can scratch your behind with your left hand.

LAMB. Sean, I'm not strong enough to hold on here.

SEAN. Johnnie'll help you. Johnnie! Hold on while I fetch Johnnie! Johnnie! (*He rushes all over the stage looking for Johnnie.*) Johnnie! Johnnie! Johnnie! He must be here somewhere! Hold on, Lamb lad, hold on! Johnnie, where the hell are you hidin'? Was he not here last night, Lamb?

LAMB. Sean, stop playing around, and let me down.

SEAN. I thought it was Johnnie you could trust.

LAMB. Johnnie wouldn't have left me up here in the first place.

SEAN. That's no excuse for him not lettin' you down. A friend in need. . . .

LAMB. Sean!

SEAN. (*singing piously*)
"Oh God our help in ages past,
Our hope that dwells aloft,
We pray thee now to help poor Lamb,
And let his fall be soft."

You know that reminds me o' the story about the Jewish father whose little boy got stuck up a tree. Do you know it? I can't do the Jewish accent, but he says "Jump, son, an' I'll catch you." An' the little boy, he says "Daddy, are you sure you won't drop me?" An' his Daddy says "Come on, son, jump." An' the little boy says, "You won't drop me, Daddy?" An' his Daddy says "Why should I drop me own son?" So the little boy jumps, an' his Daddy steps back, an' the little boy hits the ground with a terrible thud. An' he looks up at his father, tears flowin' from his eyes, an' he says "Daddy, you didn't catch me." An' his Daddy says "That'll teach you. In this world you can't trust nobody." Lovely story.

LAMB. Sean, I can't hold on much longer.

SEAN. Is it me you're askin' to help you, or Johnnie?

LAMB. You.

SEAN. All right. So long as we understand one another. (*SEAN stands below the window, and LAMB lowers himself to the ground.*) 'Tis a terrible thing to have power over another person, you know. I felt meself gettin' corrupted.

LAMB. It was a damn silly trick to play.

SEAN. It might have been from your point of view, but from mine it was good entertainment. An' that's the first worthwhile thing you've done since you came here. Well now you've looked out of the window an' done your performance on the parallel bars, how are we goin' to spend the rest of the day?

LAMB. We could look out of the other window.

SEAN. You're a glutton for punishment.

LAMB. It's your turn to go up.

SEAN. Ah no. Aha, no thank you, ole Sean can't be caught that easy. Besides, one flick o' me big toe, an' I'd be through your collar bone an' ploughin' through your ribs.

LAMB. I'd like to know what's out there.

SEAN. Are you serious?

LAMB. Yes.

SEAN. Well I'll say this for you. You've got guts. Come on, then. Up you go. (*He lifts him in the same way as last time.*) What do you see?

LAMB. It's a corridor. I suppose it's the corridor I came along yesterday. Though I didn't see all those doors.

SEAN. What doors?

LAMB. Doors. They must be other cells.

SEAN. Ah, that'll be it. Is anyone movin'?

LAMB. No, it's all still.

SEAN. Them two fellers in black aren't anywhere, are they?

LAMB. Can't see them.

SEAN. More's the better. Have you finished?

LAMB. Wait a minute. There is someone moving. Right at the end there.

SEAN. You'd better come down.

LAMB. No wait, Sean. I might be able to see him better. He's. . . .

SEAN. Come down! (*SEAN jerks him away. LAMB begins to fall in slow motion, then jumps the rest of the way.*)

LAMB. What's the matter with you? I only wanted to see who it was.

SEAN. There's nothin' to be gained from seein' what's goin' on outside. You might see somethin' that'll worry you so you can't sleep at nights. It's better to know nothin'. (*Pause*) What *did* he look like?

LAMB. I'm not sure. I think he had a beard. But he was just coming into the light when you decided to try and break my neck for me.

SEAN. Ah, another o' the bearded tribe. Lamb, never trust a man with a beard. If he's got a beard, it's ten to one he hasn't got a chin. Did you know that?

LAMB. I know that you're scared stiff of anything and everything outside this cell.

SEAN. Oh is that so?

LAMB. That is so.

SEAN. An' who was it who spent half the day yesterday dentin' the floor with his knees an' the door with his fists, and floodin' out his bed with a home-made ocean?

LAMB. That was yesterday.

SEAN. Oh yes, that was yesterday, in the year before Johnnie. 'Tis now today, anus dominoes, an' the little lamb is scared of nothin'.

LAMB. I've had time to work things out.

SEAN. An' what *have* you worked out? That what you know is useless, an' what you don't know wonderful? That the man you can touch an' talk to doesn't exist, an' the man you dream up in the dark o' night is God Almighty? Is that what you worked out?

LAMB. I worked out that it's no good trying to run away!

SEAN. Who's runnin' away? Who's runnin'? Did I shut me eyes when they took poor Jack away? Have I ever shut me eyes? Who's runnin'? I've faced them a thousand times, an' how many times have you faced them?

LAMB. You're scared all the same.

SEAN. Sure I'm scared! To hell with you! Who isn't?

LAMB. Johnnie wasn't.

SEAN. Johnnie, Johnnie, Johnnie! Will you stop throwin' Johnnie at me!

LAMB. Sean, Johnnie told me who he was.

SEAN. Johnnie told everyone who he was! Johnnie never stopped talkin' about who he was! The only bastard that ever walked into this place of his own free will — an' he walked out of it again!

LAMB. I know everything.

SEAN. You know nothin'! You know what you want to know! You're in a cell, brother. You're not in a church, an' you're not yet in the graveyard — you're in a cell, an' you can dream up all the Johnnies you fancy, but you'll not leave this cell till they come to fetch you, an' while you're here, you'll be livin' with Sean, an' Jack' an a thousand other bastards like us — an' it's with us you're livin', not with Johnnie! So give us a bit o' peace will you?

LAMB. Peace.

SEAN. Peace! On earth. An' goodwill to all men. Did you ever hear that, Lamb? Goodwill. . . .

(*There is a metallic click, and the VOICE comes over the loud-speaker:*)

VOICE. William Lamb. Cell Three. William Lamb. (*As soon as he hears this, SEAN claps his hand over his mouth.*)

SEAN. (*looking at LAMB almost with horror*) Lamb, it's you! They're comin' for you!

LAMB. (*who is scared, but fighting to keep back his fear*) I. . . . I know.

SEAN. The bastards! I'm sorry, boy. I'm sorry.

LAMB. (*muttering*) Johnnie!

SEAN. Jo. . . . Johnnie'll help you. Johnnie'll stick by you. Take it like a man, son. (*The door opens, revealing the two men in black.*) Good luck, son. (*LAMB does not resist as the two men come to either side of him.*) I didn't mean what I said just now, son. Good luck. (*The men in black take LAMB out. The door closes.*) The bastards! The damn bastards! Bastards! So they leave ole Sean on his own, eh? A dose o' the solitary. (*He lights a cigarette.*) It had to come sooner or later. Ah! The finest nerve tonic o' the lot. An' that little kid dragged off when he's hardly learnt to walk. He never fought 'em, though. Never fought 'em. Head up, chest out, like a chicken off to the slaughter. An' ole Sean's left on his own. All on his own. (*At a loss*) The declaration of independence. Arise, Sean Murphy, an' take the world by storm. (*Encouraged*) Ah well, it's a kind of freedom anyway. Beautiful thought — all this is mine. The generosity of Fate. Sean Murphy, in recognition of a lifetime's devoted livin', we present you with these four beds, these cheerful grey walls, them sweetly barred windows, an' that lovingly locked door. Long mayest thou flourish. Ah friends, friends, I am deeply touched by this honour that you do me. When I started out along the road of life, I scarcely dreamt that I should come to this great pot of gold. An' I owes it all to the many wonderful people that have stood behind me . . . an' beside me. . . . an' around me. . . . an' on top o' me. . . . in the trials an' tribulations that I have encountered tara, tara, tara. . . . He's made a good job o' these beds. He'd have made someone a lovely wife. (*Pause*) So where do we go from here, Sean boy? Where do we go from here? Let's see if the other lads are still awake. (*He goes to the door and beats on it with his fists. Imitating LAMB:*) Let me out! Let me out! Open the door! Open the door!

(*Chorus of voices from outside:* "Shut up! Belt up!" etc.)

(*Normal voice:*) Shut up! Keep quiet! (*Lamb's voice:*) Open the door! Let me out! (*Chorus from outside continues. SEAN has a quick laugh.*) Let me out! (*Our voice:*) Shut your trap! (*Lamb's voice:*) Open the door! (*The Chorus now includes a number of swear-words.*) (*Own voice:*) Shut your bloody row! Listen to 'em — like a pack o' wolves. Will you moderate your language out there! The Bishop can't stand it! Quiet! (*The row subsides.*) That's better. How can a man think with that row goin' on? There's limits to what the human ear can take. Now then, let's see what we can do. How shall we fill in the hours till bed-time? Somethin' nice an' amusin', some pleasurable occupation. To take the mind off the mind. Now what's it goin' to be? What are we goin' to do? What the hell are we goin' to do? (*Panic begins to mount.*) What's the good o' bloody talkin' when there's no-one to listen to you? They done it deliberate. To break me down. That's what they done it for. Bastards! Perhaps they'll send someone soon. They never done this before! No, no, the thing is to keep cheerful. Smile in adversity. (*Weak effort at smiling, quickly abandoned*) I'll fall back on me natural resources. (*Pause*) What natural resources? Bastards! You want me to take you on, Jack, do you? All right, let's see what you're made of. (*He squares up, just as JACK did in Act One.*) Are you ready? Heave! (*With tremendous grunting and groaning, SEAN very slowly forces the air backwards, until he is next to the left hand bunk.*) Ah! There you are! There's life in the ole dog yet. The strength of a lion, the brain of an Einstein, what more can a man desire? Lamb, that's rubbish! Rubbish! The door is locked, an' Johnnie's dead — so there couldn't have been anyone there at all, an' if there was, which there wasn't, it couldn't have been Johnnie. With one flash of me rapier-like intellect . . . one flash . . . Johnnie, if it's true, then come here, will you? Do you hear me, Johnnie? Johnnie, you bastard, I'm callin' for you! Johnnie, come here! Send someone! Let me out! Johnnie, it's the one thing I can't stand! I can't stand it, Johnnie! (*He goes to the door, and beats on it with his fists.*) Let me out o' here! Let me out o' here! (*The usual chorus.*) Johnnie, Johnnie, Johnnie, Johnnie! I got to get out! I got to get out! (*Above his cries, and the loud complaints from outside, comes a metallic click.*)

VOICE. Sean Murphy. Cell Three. Sean Murphy. (*SEAN remains on his knees at the door. The Chorus continues, and the curtain falls.*)

THE END

If Yer Take a Short Cut, Yer Might Lose the Way

a play in two scenes

CHARACTERS

FRANKIE
WILLIE
ARCHIBALD
MARTHA
JOHNNIE

SCENE: The Truthseekers' home.
TIME: Today and tomorrow.

IF YER TAKE A SHORT CUT was presented by Jimmy Wax at the Hampstead Theatre Club on February 27th 1966 with the following cast:

FRANKIE . . . . Michael Pennington
WILLIE . . . . Melvyn Hayes
ARCHIBALD . . . . John McKelvey
MARTHA . . . . Margery Withers
JOHNNIE . . . . Michael Pennington

Directed by Ian Watt-Smith
Stage Manager: Christine Roberts

If Yer Take a Short Cut

As the curtain rises, the stage is in darkness. A single spot suddenly falls on a skeleton, mid-stage. A pause of, say, five seconds, then another spot on another skeleton, stage right. Pause of five seconds, then third spot on skeleton, stage left. After a further pause, the back of the stage is lit up, revealing a huge television screen. Frankie's face appears on the screen, young, thick head of wavy black hair, greasily good-looking. He is in the middle of a song. While he sings, he smiles. We occasionally see him full length, which reveals that he is holding and playing (with) a guitar.

FRANKIE. (*singing:*)
Yeh, yeh, yeh. Yeh, yeh, yeh.
Ma baby's gone an' left me,
Yeh, yeh, yeh.
I don't know what to do,
An' I'm feelin' mighty blue,
Yeh, yeh, yeh.
Baby, oh, oh, oh,
Baby, oh, oh, oh,
Ma baby's gone an' left me,
Yeh, oh, oh, oh,
Yeh, oh, oh, oh,
Yeeeeeeeeeeeeeeeeeh. BABY!

(*There are screams and shouts from the unseen audience. FRANKIE continues to smile, and bows occasionally. He is joined on the screen by another man, who has protruding teeth and a funny face. This is WILLIE.*)

WILLIE. Oh fanks, Frankie, vat was wunnerful. Wasn't it wunnerful, folks? (*Screams and shouts*)
FRANKIE. Thank you, Willie.
WILLIE. No, fankee, Frankie. Ha, ha.

(*Laughter from audience. The set is suddenly switched off.*)

OLD FEMALE VOICE. Whatcher do that for, Archibald?
OLD MALE VOICE. Load o' rubbish. Rubbish. Load o' rubbish.

(*The rest of the stage is lit up, and we see ARCHIBALD, standing stage left, hand on light switch beside door. MARTHA is sitting in a high-backed chair front right, ARCHIBALD's chair being front left. Along the right wall, half way, is MARTHA's bed. ARCHIBALD's is directly opposite, on the left. There is no other furniture.*)

MARTHA. I wanter watch it.
ARCHIBALD. Well yer can't.
MARTHA. I want to.
ARCHIBALD. An' I don't so yer can't.
MARTHA. I'm goin' ter get a set o' controls for meself one day.
ARCHIBALD. Won't make no difference. I'm the boss. (*ARCHIBALD goes to the skeleton on the left, and we see that he is about eighty years old, with long grey hair, bent back, spectacles on the end of his nose, and a very sharp-tempered face. MARTHA remains with her back to the audience, head hidden by the high chair.*) Sooner look at me skeleton.
MARTHA. I'd sooner look at the telly.
ARCHIBALD. Heh, well yer can. It's still there!
MARTHA. I want it on.
ARCHIBALD. Well yer can't 'ave it on.
MARTHA. I want it.
ARCHIBALD. Yer can't 'ave it, so. . . . (*with great vehemence*) SHUT UP! Moanin'. 'Ave a look at yer skeleton.
MARTHA. (*miserable*) I don't wanter look at me skeleton, I want ter look at the telly.
ARCHIBALD. No truth in it.
MARTHA. There is.
ARCHIBALD. There ain't.
MARTHA. (*snivelling*) You don't care about me.
ARCHIBALD. Shut up.
MARTHA. You don't care. (*Silence*) You wouldn't care if I died. (*ARCHIBALD goes on studying his skeleton.*) Yer don't love me. (*She gets up and faces the audience. She is considerably taller than we expected, is quite bald, and is wearing dark glasses.*) Yer don't love me no more.

ARCHIBALD. Shut up moanin'. Go ter bed if yer can't shut up.

MARTHA. Bed, that's all you ever think about. Sex maniac. Why don't yer leave yer mother alone?

ARCHIBALD. She's interestin'. You ain't pretendin' you never look at yer father, are yer?

MARTHA. Not in the same way you look at yer mother. Fiddlin' with 'er pelvis.

ARCHIBALD. She's got a very nice pelvis.

MARTHA. (*mumbling*) Sex maniac. (*Silence*) Diseased. (*Silence*) Spoil other people's pleasure. (*Sudden outburst*) You never really wanted to 'ave it on in the first place, did yer? All yer really wanted was ter get back to yer skeleton, to yer rotten, stinkin' ole mother! Didn't yer! Answer me!

ARCHIBALD. There's more truth in 'er little finger than in twenty-four hours o' that rubbish. (*Vehement*) Isn't there? Eh? Answer me!

MARTHA. (*quietly*) I don't care about truth.

ARCHIBALD. That's your trouble. You won't even let me 'ave a mirror ter shave in cos yer so scared o' the truth.

MARTHA. I ain't scared of it, I just don't like it, that's all.

ARCHIBALD. So because you don't like it, I 'ave ter do without it, eh? Anyway, I'm keepin' the controls o' the telly.

MARTHA. I don't see why yer should.

ARCHIBALD. Maybe yer don't, but I'm keepin' 'em just the same. (*Silence. MARTHA slowly goes to her skeleton, while ARCHIBALD continues to examine his.*) Found anythin'?

MARTHA. Course I ain't. You'll never find anythin'.

ARCHIBALD. Yer will. It's 'idden, but it's there.

MARTHA. I'm sick o' lookin'.

ARCHIBALD. If yer found it, yer could stop lookin', couldn't yer?

MARTHA. Bloody stupid. (*Silence. MARTHA stands dejected, while ARCHIBALD goes on examining his skeleton.*)

ARCHIBALD. I 'ad an idea. S'posin' we was ter change over. You could search my mother, an' I could search yer father.

MARTHA. Blimey, now yer turnin' queer. As if I 'adn't enough troubles.

ARCHIBALD. (*vehemently*) I ain't turnin' queer. Don't bloody talk like that ter me. It was an idea. Maybe we can see into our own kind better.

MARTHA. I ain't interested in your mother.

ARCHIBALD. You ain't found nothin' in your father, 'ave yer?

MARTHA. Well?

ARCHIBALD. Well! Maybe a change'd do us both good.

MARTHA. Why don't yer 'ave a look at. . . . at. . . . (*She points to the middle skeleton.*) . . . Number Three.

ARCHIBALD. No! We'll leave 'im be.

MARTHA. Coward.

ARCHIBALD. Maybe, but I ain't losin' everything! (*Silence*) What about it, then?

MARTHA. What about what?

ARCHIBALD. (*annoyed*) What about changin'? What about me lookin' in yer dad?

MARTHA. Means we'd 'ave ter change everythin'. Beds, an' all.

ARCHIBALD. Be all right. Won't 'urt. We can always change back.

MARTHA. If yer want to. I don't mind.

ARCHIBALD. What's the matter with yer?

MARTHA. Nothin'.

ARCHIBALD. Yer plannin' somethin'.

MARTHA. I ain't.

ARCHIBALD. You better not do nothin' ter my mother. . . .

MARTHA. I won't touch 'er.

ARCHIBALD. Yer promise.

MARTHA. I promise.

ARCHIBALD. Yer up ter somethin'. What yer up to?

MARTHA. D'yer wanter change, or don't yer?

ARCHIBALD. If you do 'er any damage, so 'elp me. . . .

MARTHA. I shan't lay a finger on 'er.

ARCHIBALD. (*after momentary pause*) All right. Come on. I'll go round the back. (*He passes behind the centre skeleton, and MARTHA crosses over in front of it. Both of them make the sign of the cross when level with the centre skeleton.*) It might be interestin'. (*MARTHA sits down in ARCHIBALD's chair. ARCHIBALD, going up to the right skeleton:*) 'E don't look much different to my mother. P'raps they ain't diff'rent when they die. (*Silence*) Yer sure 'e is yer father? Looks more like yer mother. (*The television suddenly blares on, in the middle of another smiling FRANKIE tune.*) Jesus, what the 'ell. . . .

FRANKIE. (*smiling*)
   She broke my heart, yeh, heart, yer, heart,
   When she said we would part, yeh, part, yer part,
   Oh, oh, oh, oh. Yeh, yeh.
      Oh, oh, oh, oh.

ARCHIBALD. (*shouting*) Turn it off! Turn the ruddy thing off!

FRANKIE.

    Now I'm feelin' blue, yeh, blue, yeh, blue,

    An' I don't know what to do, yeh, do, yeh, do.

    Oh, oh, oh, oh. Yeh, yeh. Oh, oh, oh, oh.

ARCHIBALD. (*shouting*) Will you turn that rotten, filthy rubbish off?

MARTHA. You wanted the change. Now you can shut up. I've got the controls.

ARCHIBALD. I knew you was up to something.

FRANKIE. Join in everybody!

    She broke my heart, yeh, heart, yeh, heart,

    When she said we would part, yeh, part, yeh, part.

(*MARTHA joins in:*)

    Oh, oh, oh, oh. Yeh, yeh. Oh, oh, oh, oh.

    Now I'm feelin' blue, yeh, blue, yeh, blue,

    An' I don't know what to do, yeh, do, yeh, do,

    Oh, oh, oh, oh. Yeh, yeh, yeh. Oh, oh, oh.

(*Screams and shouts from the unseen audience. MARTHA lowers the volume.*)

MARTHA. Yer see, we missed that song. Cussed old sod. (*She sings, in a dreadful, deep, cracked voice.*)

    Now I'm feelin' blue, yeh, blue, yeh, blue,

    And I don't know what to do, yeh, do, yeh, do.

ARCHIBALD. Shut up! Shut up! Shut up! How can I work with you makin' that flamin' row?

MARTHA. Why don't yer sit down an' watch it, like everybody else does, 'stead o' nosing round them skeletons.

ARCHIBALD. I'm lookin' fer the truth.

MARTHA. You won't find nothin' there. Why don't yer enjoy yerself? (*FRANKIE has been joined by WILLIE, and now MARTHA turns the volume up again.*)

WILLIE. Fankee, Frankie, ha, ha. None o' yer hanky-panky. Ha, ha. (*Screams of laughter from the unseen audience. A deep, cracked laugh from MARTHA.*)

FRANKIE. How about you singing a song, Willie?

WILLIE. What me? Ha, ha. Silly Willie? Not on your Nilly. Ha, ha. (*More screams of laughter, plus MARTHA's gravel.*)

FRANKIE. Go on, I'll sing with you.

WILLIE. (*acting coy*) No.

FRANKIE. Go on.

WILLIE. I won't. (*Aside to camera*) I'm going to, though. We've been rehearsin' it for a month! (*Screams of laughter from unseen audience, plus MARTHA.*)

MARTHA. 'Ere, 'e's goin' ter sing. The toothy one's goin' ter sing. Why don't yer watch it, Archibald?

ARCHIBALD. Switch the flamin' thing off, an' let me get on with me work. (*She turns it up louder.*)

WILLIE. What shall we sing ven, Frankie? (*Aside to camera*) As if I didn't know. (*Screams of laughter from audience and MARTHA.*)

FRANKIE. What about Kissing and Hugging?

WILLIE. What in front of all vese people? (*A riot of laughter, plus MARTHA's witch-cackle.*)

FRANKIE. No, the song, Willie.

WILLIE. All right. You do the kissin', and leave ve huggin' to me!

(*The orchestra starts the rhythm. ARCHIBALD suddenly marches to the back of the stage and pulls out a bundle of wires. The set goes dead. MARTHA screams.*)

MARTHA. Leave it alone! Leave it alone! You bloody swine, whatcher do that for? Eh? Put it back. Put it back!

ARCHIBALD. (*slowly and deliberately*) I want ter get on with my work. An' I can't do it with that row goin' on.

MARTHA. Them wires is in this side o' the room.

ARCHIBALD. (*quickly*) No they ain't. Oh no they ain't. They're in this side o' the room. Now yer can belt up.

MARTHA. If I could reach yer I'd kill yer.

ARCHIBALD. Well yer can't, so yer can't. 'Ard cheese. (*MARTHA gets up, flings her arms wide, then lets them fall again in a gesture of helplessness.*)

MARTHA. I'd like ter kill yer! What am I goin' ter do? What am I goin' ter do?

ARCHIBALD. Why don't yer 'ave a look at my mother? Do somethin' useful with yer time, 'stead of 'anging round gawpin' at them maniacs.

MARTHA. They ain't maniacs. (*Mumbling*) Sod. Kill-joy. (*Loud*) Me eyes are 'urtin'.

ARCHIBALD. Yer shouldn't watch the telly.

MARTHA. They 'urt when I don't watch it. When I'm watchin' I don't even know I *got* eyes. Fat lot you care about anythin' or anyone! 'Cept them bloody skeletons. . . . (*turning towards the centre skeleton*). . . . savin' your grace. . . . Un'ealthy. An' you leave my Dad's what'sit alone, too, filthy-minded. . . .

ARCHIBALD. Your Dad's pelvis ain't regular in shape. Now what does that mean?

MARTHA. 'E was knocked down by a steam-roller. Don't you remember?

ARCHIBALD. But did it affect 'is character?

MARTHA. It killed 'im. I 'spect that changed 'im a bit.

ARCHIBALD. 'E never 'ad it irregular till e' got killed?

MARTHA. I never saw 'is pelvis till 'e got killed. 'E never showed it to me. I never knew 'e 'ad one till 'e 'ad it smashed. 'E probably didn't know it isself.

ARCHIBALD. It's irregular. Would you say 'e was a normal man?

MARTHA. 'E don't look too normal ter me.

ARCHIBALD. When 'e was alive!

MARTHA. Course 'e was normal. 'Course 'e was. Normal. Like everybody else.

ARCHIBALD. I'd 'ave to open 'is skull, really.

MARTHA. You ain't touchin' 'is skull. D' you 'ear? You ain't openin' nothin'. Nothin!

ARCHIBALD. It's the only way, Martha.

MARTHA. Well do it with your Mum, then.

ARCHIBALD. But I can't 'urt my Mum.

MARTHA. Well you ain't 'urtin' my Dad.

ARCHIBALD. But your Dad don't matter so much.

MARTHA. 'E does ter me. If you touch 'is skull, I'll smash yer mother's 'ead in. So take yer choice.

ARCHIBALD. I don't see 'ow I can go on. I can't make any progress till I open a skull.

MARTHA. Then open yer Mum's like I said. Or. . . . (*indicating centre skeleton*). . . . open 'is.

ARCHIBALD. (*genuinely shocked*) Martha! What are you sayin'?

MARTHA. Well don't go monkeyin' around with my Dad, that's all. 'E's 'ad enough sufferin' fer one man's eternity, without you pullin' 'is poor old skull in pieces.

ARCHIBALD. (*sulking*) I got to open somebody's skull. I can't get anywhere till I do.

MARTHA. Then give up. Or open yer Mum's. Or 'is. Or yer own.

ARCHIBALD. Yer know I can't. Yer deliberately stoppin' me from gettin' to the truth.

MARTHA. 'Ow d'you know you'd get the truth if you opened 'is skull?

ARCHIBALD. It's a chance. An' I ain't got no chance this way. I'm beaten. I got to open a skull. (*Silence*)

MARTHA. (*slowly, cunningly*) All right. I got a proposal.

ARCHIBALD. Well?

MARTHA. I'll let you open my father's skull, Archibald. . . . if. . . . (*sudden rush*). . . . you let me 'ave control o' the telly. (*Silence*)

ARCHIBALD. (*in a low voice*) Control o' the telly. (*Deep thought*) For 'ow long?

MARTHA. Always.

ARCHIBALD. No! I won't. Not for always.

MARTHA. Then you can open yer own bloody skull. 'An go to 'ell. (*Silence*)

ARCHIBALD. I'll give it ter yer fer a month.

MARTHA. Always, always, always. Or nothin' doin'.

ARCHIBALD. (*plaintively*) I'd never be able ter work, Martha. I can't work with the telly on.

MARTHA. Yer can't work without a skull to open.

ARCHIBALD. But Martha, you'd 'ave it on all day an' night, wouldn't yer?

MARTHA. Yes, I would.

ARCHIBALD. 'ow could I work?

MARTHA. (*business-like*) Without openin' the skull, yer can't get at the truth, can yer?

ARCHIBALD. No.

MARTHA. Now if yer was to open the skull, an' yer got the truth, yer'd 'ave finished yer work, wouldn't yer?

ARCHIBALD. (*working it out*) Yes.

MARTHA. So if yer'd finished yer work, yer'd 'ave nothin' left ter do but watch the telly — so you wouldn't be any the worse off.

ARCHIBALD. (*again after working it out*) Supposin' I don't find nothin'?

MARTHA. Then you won't never get the truth, 'cos there ain't nothin' left ter try. Yer'll still 'ave ter watch telly.

ARCHIBALD. (*with a touch of despair*) There must be somethin' else.

MARTHA. What?

ARCHIBALD. Somethin'.

MARTHA. You know what your trouble is?

ARCHIBALD. What?

MARTHA. You're scared to open a skull, that's what.

ARCHIBALD. Scared? Me?

MARTHA. Scared. You. Yer know why? 'Cos yer scared yer won't find anythin', that's why.

ARCHIBALD. It ain't true.

MARTHA. It's true.

ARCHIBALD. It ain't.

MARTHA. Scared yer won't find anythin'. An' if you ain't scared yer won't find anythin', yer scared that yer will. It's all the same in the end.

ARCHIBALD. All I want is the truth.

MARTHA. Balls.

ARCHIBALD. Don't be vulgar.

MARTHA. Ho, ho, don't be vulgar. Sudden rise in the scale, eh? Since when was you concerned about vulgarity? Muckin' around with yer mother's pelvis.

ARCHIBALD. I'm lookin' fer the truth!

MARTHA. If yer lookin' fer the truth, then why don't you cut 'im open? (*indicating centre skeleton*)

ARCHIBALD. We got to leave 'im alone.

MARTHA. Why?

ARCHIBALD. Cos 'e's 'oly.

MARTHA. Who says?

ARCHIBALD. I noticed you bloody crossed yerself when you passed in front of 'im. In spite of all yer bravado (*pronounced bravverdo*)

MARTHA. I'm coverin' meself, that's all. Don't mean I'm 'is slave.

ARCHIBALD. Well, I ain't cuttin' 'im open, an' that's flat.

MARTHA. You know my terms. Take 'em or leave 'em.

ARCHIBALD. I ain't 'avin the telly on all the rest of me life.

MARTHA. What's wrong with the telly?

ARCHIBALD. (*rather pathetically*) Martha, I wanter be 'uman.

MARTHA. Meanin' what?

ARCHIBALD. 'Uman. 'Uman. Alive. Real. (*Silence*) Martha, I wanter come back ter me mother. (*Silence*) Did you 'ear me?

MARTHA. I 'eard yer.

ARCHIBALD. Well?

MARTHA. Well what?

ARCHIBALD. (*vehemently*) I wanter come back ter me mother!

MARTHA. Only if I 'ave control o' the telly.

ARCHIBALD. No, that was fer yer Dad's skull.

MARTHA. It's fer this, too. I want control o' the telly.

ARCHIBALD. But Martha, yer can't do this. It ain't fair.

MARTHA. I want the telly, I want the telly, I want the telly! You ain't got no right ter take it away from me! No right, d'you 'ear? I got a right to the telly, an' you ain't got the right to take it away from me. (*She is very upset.*) I live for the telly. That's all I got ter live for in this rotten dump. An' you take it away from me.

ARCHIBALD. But it ain't the truth.

MARTHA. I don't want the truth. I want the telly! And now me eyes is half killin' me. What d'you expect me ter do all day long?

ARCHIBALD. You could 'elp me in my work.

MARTHA. I don't want to 'elp you in yer work. I 'ate it. I can't stand the way you look at them bones. It ain't nat'ral.

ARCHIBALD. When we was married you promised fer better or fer worse.

MARTHA. I know. But I never expected it ter be the worse. You promised ter look after me.

ARCHIBALD. Well, I 'ave done. I bought yer the telly, didn't I?

MARTHA. An' now yer won't let me look at it. (*Wailing*) An' it's my fav'rite programme too!

ARCHIBALD. But your fav'rite programme's on fer twenty-four hours a day. You never wanter stop.

MARTHA. Well, I'm 'appy when I'm watchin' it.

ARCHIBALD. But where does it get yer? I mean, what's the point of it all?

MARTHA. What's the point of lookin' at yer Mum all day?

ARCHIBALD. (*annoyed*) I'm looking fer the truth, that's what. The truth! An' what are you lookin' for, watchin' that ruddy machine.

MARTHA. Happiness.

ARCHIBALD. (*after a short silence*) Happiness. From that?

MARTHA. Yes. (*Dreamily*) Seein' Frankie, with 'is wavy 'air—adorable Frankie. An' Willie, with 'is lovely 'umour—lovable Willie. Seein' the people dancin', an' makin' love, an' killin' one another, an' singin', an fightin', an' killin' one another. An' the news every day, with all the fightin' an' killin', an' the Queen, an' the politicians, an' the dancin' and the nice plays, an' Frankie an' Willie. They all make you 'appy.

ARCHIBALD. (*gently*) I know, Martha, it's nice an' all that. But where does it get you?

MARTHA. Nowhere. Like lookin' at yer Mum.

ARCHIBALD. My Mum's dead.

MARTHA. Well, then.

ARCHIBALD. The truth must be there.

MARTHA. You'll get the truth anyway, sooner or later, Archibald, won't you? Face facts. You'll get it sooner or later.

ARCHIBALD. I want it now. (*Silence*)

MARTHA. Well I don't see that that gives you the right to rob me of my telly. (*Silence*)

ARCHIBALD. It was a mistake for us to 'ave got married in the first place. I should 'ave married a woman who looked on life the same way as I do.

MARTHA. Maybe you should 'ave done.

ARCHIBALD. P'raps I should 'ave married me mother. She an' I always understood each other. We 'ad a wonderful understandin'. I'll never forgive 'er for dyin' like that. It was a mistake ter marry you. P'raps I should 'ave married 'er.

MARTHA. Or stayed single.

ARCHIBALD. I might 'ave got lonely if I'd stayed single. An' anyway, I wouldn't 'ave 'ad someone else's skull to open then, would I?

MARTHA. You 'aven't got my Dad's yet.

ARCHIBALD. No, but it's the possibility that's important. E's there. That's what matters.

MARTHA. An' I don't matter, I s'pose.

ARCHIBALD. You *do* matter, Martha. You mean a lot to me. I wouldn't 'ave anyone ter talk to if you wasn't there. It's terrible ter be alone, yer know — it's almost the worst thing that can 'appen to yer. No-one ter talk to, no-one ter converse with, no-one there in the mornin's, when yer get up, no-one ter say goodnight to when yer get down. Yer see these ole women what ain't got no 'usbands, they wait in the doorway, they wait, 'opin' someone'll come along, so they can talk a bit. Yer can never get away from them once they start, an' it's only because they're lonely, yer know. They ain't got no-one ter talk to. Terrible when yer see them women, all shrivelled up with loneliness. Oh yes, yer got a lot ter be thankful for, Martha. There's plenty worse off than you.

MARTHA. We wasn't talkin' about me, we was talkin' about you.

ARCHIBALD. No, Martha, I was talkin', an' I was talkin' about you. You ain't done so bad, bein' married ter me. I've treated you all right. Bought you a telly. We got a nice 'ome, comfortable furniture. An' I even let you bring yer father 'ere, didn't I? I didn't 'ave to, you know.

MARTHA. You only let me bring 'im cos you wanted to cut 'is skull open.

ARCHIBALD. That may be partly true, but I let you put 'im up there, 'avin' equal importance to my Mum. Not many 'usbands would do that. You ain't done so bad.

MARTHA. I could 'ave done better.

ARCHIBALD. Oh? 'Ow d'you make that out?

MARTHA. I 'ad offers.

ARCHIBALD. Who from?

MARTHA. Never you mind. I 'ad 'em.

ARCHIBALD. You never did!

MARTHA. Yes, I did. Don't you tell me I didn't when I did. I 'ad offers. Important people, too.

ARCHIBALD. In yer dreams, most likely.

MARTHA. There was a very rich man what was after me.

ARCHIBALD. Stolen 'is money, 'ad yer?

MARTHA. 'Is name was Sir Charles. (*Silence*)

ARCHIBALD. Go on.

MARTHA. 'E owned a yacht, an' a fleet o' cars, an' e' 'ad a castle in the South of France. 'E was after me.

ARCHIBALD. But yer turned 'im down.

MARTHA. Yes. An' there was a cowboy, what 'ad six-shooters round 'is waist. 'E wanted me too. An'. . . . an'. . . . an' a news announcer. . . .

ARCHIBALD. Dreams.

MARTHA. They wasn't dreams. I tell yer, they was all after me. I was much sought after.

ARCHIBALD. Like 'ell you was.

MARTHA. I 'ad golden 'air, an' blue eyes. I was a lovely girl.

ARCHIBALD. Why did yer turn 'em down, then?

MARTHA. (*stumped for quite a time*) Well. . . . I wasn't ready then.

ARCHIBALD. Ready fer what?

MARTHA. Marryin'. I wasn't ready. An' I didn't love any of 'em.

ARCHIBALD. And then yer met me.

MARTHA. Yes.

ARCHIBALD. The first man what you ever loved. I swept you off yer feet. An' carried you off on me milk white steed. You, an' yer Dad.

MARTHA. If I'd known then what I know now, I'd 'ave married one of them, an' let you go to 'ell.

ARCHIBALD. Would you, Martha?

MARTHA. Yes, I would. (*Silence*) I might 'ave lived 'appy ever after then. With no regrets.

ARCHIBALD. You ain't done so bad with me, Martha. You ain't done so bad. I'm the one with regrets.

MARTHA. You? What 'ave you got to regret?

ARCHIBALD. Everythin'. Failure. Blindness. . . .

MARTHA. You ain't blind!

ARCHIBALD. Of the spirit. A life spent in fruitless endeavour, as they say in the best books. The vain search fer truth. I'm a man what's been sacrificed on the altar of . . . of. . . . a man what's given 'is life ter the pursuit of the truth. . . . the grail. . . . an' been baulked at every turn. I've given my life to the pursuit of truth. . . . an' I've been. . . . baulked. . . . at every turn.

MARTHA. (*joining in*) At every turn.

≈ ARCHIBALD. An' I've 'ad no 'elp. Not from you, not from no-one. Alone I've 'ad to struggle on, resistin' every temptation ter give up; resistin' the call of the telly. Resistin' the great 'indrance that calls 'erself me wife. Me help-mate. You! I'm a bloody martyr.

MARTHA. If yer all that keen, why don't yer kill yerself, an' find out that way?

ARCHIBALD. If yer take a short cut, yer might lose the way.

MARTHA. 'Ere, that's quite good. You should send that up somewhere.

ARCHIBALD. Whatcher mean?

MARTHA. If yer take a short cut, yer might lose the way. Send it up somewhere. They pay fer things like that.

ARCHIBALD. Who do?

MARTHA. I dunno. People what use them. They pay for things like that, they do, I know. It's important. They might even perform it on the telly.

ARCHIBALD. I made it up.

MARTHA. I know yer did.

ARCHIBALD. Well, 'ow can they perform it?

MARTHA. They'll buy it from yer. They might even ask yer ter perform it yerself.

ARCHIBALD. What? On the telly?

MARTHA. Yes.

ARCHIBALD. (*rather taken with the idea, in spite of himself*) On the telly. Me? What would I do?

MARTHA. You'd 'ave ter recite it.

ARCHIBALD. Just like that?

MARTHA. Thousands of people would watch yer. Yer'd be famous.

ARCHIBALD. Famous? Sounds all right. What do I 'ave ter do?

MARTHA. I dunno. We could 'phone 'em up.

ARCHIBALD. Who?

MARTHA. The Television people.

ARCHIBALD. We don't know their number.

MARTHA. I do. I got it writ down. 'ere. (*She pulls a piece of paper from her bosom.*)

ARCHIBALD. The phone's on your side.

MARTHA. I'll phone 'em. You ain't gettin' 'ere as easy as that. What was it again? If yer take a short cut. . . .

ARCHIBALD. Yer might lose the way. It's clever orl right. Oh, it's clever.

MARTHA. I won't tell it to 'em, though. I'll just say we got somethin' they could use. Tickle up their int'rest.

ARCHIBALD. I wouldn't mind goin' on the telly for a bit. (*MARTHA pulls the phone out from under the chair, and begins to dial.*)

ARCHIBALD. People like me deserve fame. People what 'ave devoted their lives ter the truth. A bit o' fame wouldn't do me no 'arm. You ain't done so bad with me, Martha. Security, a 'ome, an' the wife of a man what's made 'is name. D'you 'ear? Who yer phonin'?

MARTHA. 'Allo. Zat the Television people? I'm number four million nine 'undred an' seventy-six. Yes, it's paid for. (*She looks at ARCHIBALD.*) They're puttin' me through. (*Silence*) 'Allo, yes, that's right. (*To ARCHIBALD*) Still puttin' me through. Oh, hallo. (*Her voice suddenly becomes surprisingly smooth, and fetching.*) Hallo. Yes, that is correct, four million, naine hundred and seventy six. I'm very well, thank you. . . . You have a nice voice too. . . . Why thank you. . . . Hmmm-mmm! Well you see I have something I think you might be able to make use of. . . . yes, on the television, oho, oho, what did you think I meant, you naughty man? . . . that's right. . . . yes, of course you can come over. You know the house, don't you,

you've been on our screen so many times! . . . Yes, you come, dear. Yes, bring your friend too. You come . . . Byeeeee. (*She rings off, and resumes with her normal voice.*) They're comin'.

ARCHIBALD. Who's comin'?

MARTHA. Them. The telly people. Our gods are comin'.

ARCHIBALD. 'Ere?

MARTHA. Yes.

ARCHIBALD. Why, Martha? Why?

MARTHA. (*vehemently*) Cos I wanted them to come. I wanted them. *I* wanted. I desired to 'ave my will. My telly people are comin'. 'Ere. They're comin' 'ere. I gave the order, I set the wheels of the events rollin', and now the great ones are comin' 'ere. D'you understand? Do you? *I, I, I* gave the order!

ARCHIBALD. An' whose great thought was it that started this process? Whose thought?

MARTHA. You never knew. Did yer? You'd 'ave let it go, an' it'd 'ave been lost. It took *my* brain ter pick up the gold from what you ACCIDENTALLY let slip. *I*'m the one what recernized the value of what you said. (*This dispute becomes increasingly vehement.*)

ARCHIBALD. *I* said it.

MARTHA. An' I knew what it was.

ARCHIBALD. There would 'ave bin nothin' without *my* original thought. You're just actin' like the agent ter the genius.

MARTHA. Genius!

ARCHIBALD. (*shouting*) GENIUS! Genius, genius! What other man 'as bin able ter grapple life-long with the truth? (*With huge emphasis*) What other man. . . . in the *world*. . . . ever thought of studyin' the remains o' the dead. . . . in order ter find. . . . the soul? In later times, Martha, when the truth is known, they'll speak my name with awe—WITH *A W E!* An' in the midst o' these great endeavours, I find time still ter create new expressions, new thoughts about life. Even the telly people are after me. D'you 'ear? What d'yer say ter that?

MARTHA. *I* phoned up the telly people.

ARCHIBALD. Because the phone is on your side! No other reason. By chance, the phone is on your side. Otherwise, *I* would 'ave phoned them up.

MARTHA. I suggested phonin' 'em up.

ARCHIBALD. Lie! Delib'rate lie!

MARTHA. *I* suggested it.

ARCHIBALD. Who thought o' the thought?

MARTHA. (*at the top of her voice*) You thought it, I recernized it! *I* changed our lives! *I* did!

ARCHIBALD. If a King gives a loaf of bread to a beggar, which of the two is the greater?

MARTHA. Balls!

ARCHIBALD. Answer! Answer!

MARTHA. Completely off the subject.

ARCHIBALD. Yer can't answer. Yer can't, cos yer daren't.

MARTHA. The king.

ARCHIBALD. Exactly.

MARTHA. Exactly what?

ARCHIBALD. I am the king. My words are the bread. An' *you* are the beggar.

MARTHA. Kid yourself. Kid yourself. If there's a diamond necklace in a holler tree-trunk, an' it's found by a saint, who is the richer an' greater?

ARCHIBALD. Than what?

MARTHA. What?

ARCHIBALD. Than what?

MARTHA. Don't follow.

ARCHIBALD. Richer an' greater than what?

MARTHA. I'll explain it to yer. *You* are the tree, the thought is the necklace, an' I'm the saint. I'm the greater.

ARCHIBALD. Typical of women. No logic. No reason. You're a fool, Martha. Never 'ad a wise thought in yer life. Never 'ad a thought like mine, that comes shinin' up from the depths like a gleamin' pearl. My thought will enrich the earth. You'll see me on telly, Martha, an' you'll know—the man you're privileged ter be wedded to is enlightenin' the world.

MARTHA. With one measly thought.

ARCHIBALD. It's a deep thought. Deep.

MARTHA. What was it?

ARCHIBALD. What was what?

MARTHA. The thought? (*Silence*)

ARCHIBALD. The thought, Martha, I've forgot it. Martha, think 'ard. What was it?

MARTHA. I don't remember. I don't remember. (*A door bell chimes, to the tune of Beethoven's Seventh, Second Movement.*) The door! It's them!

ARCHIBALD. Don't let them in.

MARTHA. I must. It's them.

ARCHIBALD. We've forgotten the thought.

MARTHA. They must be let in, the great ones. Their entrance cannot be denied.

ARCHIBALD. No, Martha, not yet, not yet!

MARTHA. At once. If we let them go, we'll be condemned fer ever. At once!

(*She flings open the door, and WILLIE enters, followed by FRANKIE.*)

WILLIE. Good afternoon sir. Is your wife at home? (*He pushes roughly past MARTHA. ARCHIBALD has turned his back to the door, and WILLIE marches up to him.*) Ugh, grey hair. Good afternoon, Madam. (*Louder!*) Good afternoon. (*ARCHIBALD turns round, and WILLIE is shocked.*)

ARCHIBALD. (*pointing at MARTHA*) That's the wife.

WILLIE. Oh! Oh, I see.

MARTHA. You're Willie.

WILLIE. Yes.

MARTHA. An' you're Frankie.

FRANKIE. Yes.

WILLIE. Now, Mr. . . . Mrs. Truth-Seeker (*Aside to FRANKIE*) Not much doin' 'ere, unless you want 'im. (*Louder to MARTHA*) You rang us. On the telephone.

MARTHA. I admire you, Willie. An' you, Frankie.

WILLIE. We've noticed you switch on regularly. You're good viewers. You rang. What was it for?

MARTHA. We 'ave somethin' for you.

WILLIE. What?

MARTHA. A thought. For your lovely programme.

WILLIE. A thought! It's dangerous.

MARTHA. It's not dangerous. It's harmless. Tell them, Archibald. (*Silence*) Archibald, your thought.

ARCHIBALD. (*inspired*) No! No, it must be guarded. Till we're sure it'll be properly treated. I want payment first. Guarantees.

WILLIE. My dear Truth-Seeker, it is you who pay us!

MARTHA. What? What's the fee?

WILLIE. Usually, one night. But in your case, I think we'll waive it.

MARTHA. (*aside to FRANKIE*) I'd pay you, Frankie. A night.

WILLIE. Frankie takes the men. I take the women. (*To FRANKIE, indicating ARCHIBALD*) D'you want him?

FRANKIE. No. I'm not desperate.

WILLIE. You see. Give us the thought.

ARCHIBALD. I'm comin' on the programme.

WILLIE. I decide that.

ARCHIBALD. If you want the thought, I come with it. No me, no thought.

WILLIE. You can't dictate to me.

ARCHIBALD. (*suddenly very subservient*) I ain't dictatin' to yer, sir. I ain't dictatin'. Believe me I never would. My wife'll tell yer, I never dictate. I'm the 'umble kind. I watch you every day, sir, every day. I belong to the brother'ood. When I say I'm comin' on the programme, I mean. . . . I believe in yer. I'm one o' the brother'ood. I understand the values, like. An' my thought is just a contribution. . . . to reality.

FRANKIE. (*to WILLIE*) He's quite a sweet old man, really.

WILLIE. You getting keen?

FRANKIE. Possibly. Don't let on yet.

WILLIE. (*wandering round the room, determined to change the subject*) Nice skeletons you have here. Well preserved. How come you have three?

MARTHA. The centre one's Archibald's. He will insist, you know.

WILLIE. Are the authorities aware that you have three?

ARCHIBALD. (*very hesitant*) Er. . . . no sir, not exactly!

WILLIE. Running a risk, aren't you? You could be in serious trouble you know.

ARCHIBALD. I know, sir. . . . but I'm old, you see. . . . I'm partly in the past.

WILLIE. In spite of what the Government says?

ARCHIBALD. I believe in the Government, too. I'm a member of the Party.

WILLIE. Then why three?

ARCHIBALD. It's. . . . it's. . . . for a scientific investigation. I'm a historian. You see, I'm going to cut open the skull and investigate. Find out what caused those old ideas, you know.

WILLIE. It's dangerous. You could be in trouble.

ARCHIBALD. Yes, but when I publish my thesis, the Government'll be grateful. It'll be proof, yer see.

WILLIE. So you say. (*Slight pause*) Anyway, who needs proof? Are you suggesting it hasn't been proved? Is that what you're suggesting?

ARCHIBALD. Oh no, no, sir, not at all. No, not at all, No. Definitely not, sir, no. Oh, no no, no.

WILLIE. Then what do we need proof for?

MARTHA. (*with sudden urgency*) Don't answer, Archibald! Willie, we sent for you because Archibald has had a thought, which would be very good for your programme. That's why we sent for you, because of Archibald's beautiful thought.

FRANKIE. We haven't heard the thought yet.

MARTHA. Ah! That's the treat in store.

WILLIE. What's the thought?

MARTHA. We both want to go on the telly. If you promise us we can go on the telly, we'll let you know what the thought is.

ARCHIBALD. I'm to go on the telly. Me. Not you. Me.

MARTHA. Both of us, my dear.

ARCHIBALD. No, me alone, me. Alone. I'm to go on the telly, not you. It's my thought.

MARTHA. I spotted it.

ARCHIBALD. It's my thought! Me alone on the telly.

MARTHA. Me with. Me.

ARCHIBALD. No.

MARTHA. Me with.

ARCHIBALD. Me on me own.

MARTHA. (*vehemently, to WILLIE*) Who telephoned you? Eh? Who telephoned?

WILLIE. It sounded like a woman.

MARTHA. Me. It was me!

ARCHIBALD. It don't matter who phoned. You only phoned cos the phone was on your side. It's the thought that matters. The thought!

MARTHA. I. . . .

ARCHIBALD. The thought! The thought! The thought! The thought! The thought! (*She tries to interrupt, but he shouts her down.*)

WILLIE. (*shouting even louder*) Well, what is the bloody thought? (*Silence; quieter*) What is the bloody thought?

MARTHA. No need to swear. (*To ARCHIBALD*) Well what is the bloody thought? (*Silence. Both strive to remember.*)

FRANKIE. A fine evening's entertainment they'll give the fans.

WILLIE. Whichever of you remembers the thought first will appear on the telly. And if you can't remember it in five minutes, neither of you'll be on.

ARCHIBALD. (*racking his brains*) The thought.

MARTHA. (*ditto*) The thought! (*Long silence*)

ARCHIBALD. It's a long road that 'as no endin'.

FRANKIE. Blimey!

WILLIE. Cliché! Don't waste our time!

MARTHA. Somethin' ter do with air.

WILLIE. Air?

FRANKIE. Something like "He who stops breathing dies".

MARTHA. (*cackling*) Oh Frankie, you are funny. That's really funny. I admire you ever so much. (*Quieter*) Are yer sure yer wouldn't like to 'ave me?

FRANKIE. Ugh!

MARTHA. 'E keeps me imprisoned 'ere. 'E's a monster. Take me away from 'ere, Frankie. I'll be your slave.

ARCHIBALD. I got it! I got the thought. I shall come on the telly. I've remembered it, clear an' bright like it just come ter me. All new an' shinin'. D'yer wanner 'ear it?

WILLIE. Tell us then.

ARCHIBALD. Do I come on?

WILLIE. If it's any good.

ARCHIBALD. You said I could come on. I can or I can't?

WILLIE. (*to FRANKIE*) D'you want him?

FRANKIE. (*to WILLIE*) No, but let him come on if it's any good. It'll get us a reputation for charity when they come to write our life-stories.

WILLIE. All right, you're on. What's the thought?

ARCHIBALD. (*after dramatic pause*) If yer take a short cut, yer might lose the way. (*Silence*) Well. 'Ow about it?

WILLIE. It's all right.

ARCHIBALD. When do I come on?

WILLIE. (*looking at his watch*) Who's on now? Switch it on, will you?

ARCHIBALD. Yes, sir, of course. (*He rushes over to the wires, and plugs in. Then he realizes the switch is on MARTHA's side. Moment of panic. To FRANKIE:*) Er, the switch is just by you, under the chair. (*MARTHA looks daggers at him. FRANKIE switches on. When the set warms up, we see FRANKIE on the screen.*)

MARTHA. 'Ere, Frankie, it's you! It's you, my darlin'. . . .

FRANKIE. (*on the screen*)

Dreamin', dreamin', dreamin' of you-ou-ou.

I don't know, don't know, don't know what to do-o-o-o. . . .

MARTHA. How d'yer do it? Up there, an' down 'ere? 'Ow, Frankie, tell us.

FRANKIE. (*on screen*)
Yer left me, left me, left me so blue-ue-ue,
And now all day I'm dreamin' dreamin' of you.
Baby of you.

MARTHA. 'Ow, Frankie? Tell us.

WILLIE. He's got a split personality. Ha, ha, that's good, eh Frankie? A split personality. We can use that one. Next show. Split personality.

ARCHIBALD. When do I come on?

WILLIE. All right, turn it off now. (*To ARCHIBALD*) Turn it off.

ARCHIBALD. Martha, turn it off.

MARTHA. I won't. You don't want it off, do yer Frankie? (*FRANKIE turns it off.*) Oh Frankie! Why d'yer do that?

FRANKIE. Shut your ugly gob!

WILLIE. Split personality. I like it. It's good. (*To ARCHIBALD*) Now, what was the thought?

ARCHIBALD. The thought. Ah, it's gone again. I lost it.

FRANKIE. If you take a short cut, you might lose the way.

ARCHIBALD. Yes, that's it. If yer take a short cut, yer might lose the way.

WILLIE. Tomorrow. We'll put you on tomorrow. Come to the studio at six o'clock tomorrow morning. (*Going to FRANKIE*) Do you want him?

FRANKIE. No.

WILLIE. Right, let's go. Goodbye.

MARTHA. Goodbye.

ARCHIBALD. Goodbye. Tomorrow.

MARTHA. Goodbye, Frankie. (*FRANKIE and WILLIE have gone.*)

ARCHIBALD. A star. That's me, a star, on the telly. A star! Fame at last. Recernition. Ha, no flies on Arch. I'm a great man. D'yer hear that, father-in-law, you ole bum? I'm a great man. (*He gives the skeleton a slap on the pelvis, and it falls to the ground with a crash. There is a horrified silence.*)

MARTHA. You bastard. You bastard. You bleedin' bloody bastard. (*She rushes to the skeleton on her side, and viciously strikes it so that it falls.*) An' that's fer yer mother.

ARCHIBALD. I wanner change sides! Martha, I wanner come ter me mother.

MARTHA. Come on then. (*With violent haste, they cross over,*

ARCHIBALD behind and MARTHA in front of the third skeleton. Each of them makes the sign of the cross, then hurries to his skeleton.)

ARCHIBALD. (*staring in horror*) Yer've bust 'er skull. Yer've bust it.

MARTHA. Me dad's pelvis. Yer've split it in two. Bastard!

ARCHIBALD. (*becoming interested*) Yer've bust 'er skull, an'. . . . an' there's nothin' in it. There's nothin' there. It's empty. Martha, there's nothin' there.

MARTHA. There's nothin' in me dad's pelvis either.

ARCHIBALD. Nothin' there. So where is it? That's the question. Where is it?

THE CURTAIN FALLS

END OF SCENE ONE

SCENE TWO

*The following evening. The two skeletons have been repaired —
    ARCHIBALD's mother with an enormous piece of pink
    sticking-plaster across her skull, MARTHA's father with an
    equally enormous piece of blue sticking-plaster over his pel-
    vis. ARCHIBALD and MARTHA are both in their respec-
    tive chairs, with their backs to the audience. There is a long
    silence.*

ARCHIBALD. Go on.

MARTHA. No. (*Silence*)

ARCHIBALD. I wish you was dead.

MARTHA. I don't care. I don't see why you should 'ave all the fun.

ARCHIBALD. Just let me watch meself. Please Martha! (*Silence*) Frankie might be on.

MARTHA. I don't care 'bout Frankie no more.

ARCHIBALD. (*venomously*) Just 'cos 'e wouldn't sleep wiv yer! Lost yer charms, ain't yer. (*MARTHA gets up, swings her chair round to face the audience, and sits down again.*)

MARTHA. I never wanter see 'em again. (*Silence*) Bastard. (*Silence*) Bloody bastard. (*Silence*) Frankie, ugh! (*Vehemently*) Now I've seen 'im I wouldn't even wanter sleep wiv 'im! They can keep 'im. 'E don't even 'ave sex-appeal. (*ARCHIBALD gets up, and carries his chair right to the centre. He puts it down to face MARTHA, sideways on to the audience, and sits again.*)

ARCHIBALD. Martha. Let's just 'ave it on fer my bit. Just fer my bit. Please.

MARTHA. Yer really want it, don't yer?

ARCHIBALD. Yes.

MARTHA. Well, yer can't ave it. You 'ad them wires out when I wanted it on; now yer can 'ave a dose of yer own med'cine.

ARCHIBALD. Martha this is diff'rent. This is me. Yer've never seen me before.

MARTHA. Never seen yer! Blimey, I've bin lookin' at yer all me life. Why should yer be any better on the telly than y'are now? (*Silence*)

ARCHIBALD. Frankie was.

MARTHA. Frankie was what?

ARCHIBALD. Better on the telly than in real life. You loved 'im on the telly.

MARTHA. So what?

ARCHIBALD. Well, yer loved 'im on the telly, but yer didn't love 'im in real life, didn't yer? Or did yer? I mean, it might be the same wiv me, or the other way round.

MARTHA. Yer don't think I c'd fall fer you, do yer?

ARCHIBALD. It's a chance, ain't it? Somethin' to 'ope for.

MARTHA. (*melodramatically*) All 'ope is gorn. There ain't no 'ope no more. Frankie, Willie, the telly, my dad, your mum. What's left? Apart from 'im (*indicating centre skeleton*).

ARCHIBALD. You included the telly, Martha, but we ain't finished wiv the telly.

MARTHA. I 'ave. Finished! I never wanter see it again. I 'ope it rots!

ARCHIBALD. (*after reflective pause*) I thought Willie was lookin' at you in a funny way.

MARTHA. (*interested, despite herself*) Whatcher mean?

ARCHIBALD. 'E was looking at yer, in a funny way. I nearly socked 'im when I saw 'im.

MARTHA. 'Ow was 'e lookin' at me?

ARCHIBALD. Funny. Like you was a woman.

MARTHA. I am a woman! I am!

ARCHIBALD. Yes, you are. I think 'e was noticin'. I nearly socked 'im.

MARTHA. You couldn't sock a foot! Where was 'e lookin' then?

ARCHIBALD. All over.

MARTHA. Yer kiddin'.

ARCHIBALD. I ain't. I didn't like it, I can tell yer. If 'e does it again, I might do somethink e'll regret. (*Slowly MARTHA gets up, and goes to the back of the room. She plugs in the wires. ARCHIBALD gives a huge grin when she's not looking, and switches on. WILLIE's face appears on the screen.*)

WILLIE. An' vat was Mr. Trufseeker an' his wonderful fought! Well done. . . .

ARCHIBALD. We've missed it! We've missed it!

WILLIE. An' now it's time. . . .

ARCHIBALD. We missed me! All cos of you!

WILLIE. . . . for Frankie an' anuvver of his lovely songs.

ARCHIBALD. I missed meself on the telly! Me great moment!

MARTHA. Shut up, I wanner 'ear what Willie's sayin'.

WILLIE. Come on, Frankie. (*FRANKIE appears with WILLIE on the screen.*)

MARTHA. (*standing before the screen, making signals to WILLIE*) 'Ere I am, Willie. Look, 'ere!

WILLIE. Vat was a nice fought, wan't it, Frankie?

MARTHA. 'E ain't lookin' at me.

ARCHIBALD. We missed my thought.

FRANKIE. It was, Willie. Good and wise, that thought.

WILLIE. Yeah, what you might call a wisecrack, eh? (*Shrieks of laughter from the unseen audience*)

MARTHA. 'E ain't lookin' at me no'ow, let alone funny.

ARCHIBALD. Me first appearance ever, an' we missed it, all cos of your bloody interferin'. (*Viciously he switches off the set.*)

MARTHA. Oh! Whatcher do that for?

ARCHIBALD. Cos I've finished. We missed me.

MARTHA. I wanner watch Willie.

ARCHIBALD. Willie can go to 'ell.

MARTHA. I wanter see if 'e's lookin' at me.

ARCHIBALD. 'E ain't.

MARTHA. Whatcher mean 'e ain't?

ARCHIBALD. 'E ain't lookin at yer.

MARTHA. Yer said 'e was.

ARCHIBALD. 'E never was. Why should 'e look at a miserable sack o' rubbish like you?

MARTHA. You said 'e looked at me funny.

ARCHIBALD. So would anybody. If yer could see yerself, you'd look at yerself funny too. Yer 'orrible. Now belt up!

MARTHA. Willie was after me, an' you're just jealous. That's what it is.

ARCHIBALD. Jealous! If the bloody dog was after yer I'd pay 'im ter take yer.

MARTHA. Just talkin' fer the sake of talkin', you are. You know as well as I do Willie was after me. I felt 'is eyes on me all the time 'e was 'ere. Desirin' me, 'e was. Desirin'. Them eyes was burnin' through me dress.

ARCHIBALD. Yeah, an' them teeth was fallin' over one anuvver ter find the way out.

MARTHA. You ain't puttin' me off as easy as that, Archibald. All my life I've waited fer true love, all my life I've dreamed of someone strong an' powerful. What would sweep me off me feet. Why d'yer think I've watched the telly all these years? Eh? Answer me that? Fer love, that's what! Ter find a man what would be brave enough an' strong enough to deserve my love.

ARCHIBALD. 'E'd 'ave ter be brave all right.

MARTHA. An' now I've found 'im. Willie. I always knew it'd be 'im. Always. The moment I set eyes on 'im. I knew 'e was the man fer me. I pretended it was Frankie I was after; I knew that'd make Willie jealous, an' 'e'd 'ave ter bring 'is love out inter the open. 'E's a shy un is Willie, needs forcin' along. But it's 'im I love, it's Willie. I confess it. I'm in love wiv Willie. An' now yer tryin' ter takin 'im away from me. You, wiv yer insane jealousy, yer mad jealous rages, but love won't be denied, it won't. No force on earth can keep Willie an' me apart. Faith can move mountains. Telly, I command you to come on! (*Silence. She stands before the screen, willing it to come on. It does not.*) Telly, by the force of my will, I order you ter come on.

ARCHIBALD. 'Ow can it come on when it's switched off?

MARTHA. If yer got faith, yer can do these things.

ARCHIBALD. Faith! Since when 'as there bin anythin' to 'ave faith in? (*MARTHA walks to the centre skeleton, and kneels before it.*)

MARTHA. Please, Lord, let the telly come on, an' let Willie love me truly. 'ear my prayer, Lord, even though the Government forbids it, an' 'ave pity on me in my un'appiness. An' 'ave pity on my husband too, who's also un'appy. Let the telly come on, an' let Willie love me truly. (*ARCHIBALD, very moved, deliberately picks up the controls, and switches on the television.*) Please Lord. (*FRANKIE appears, singing and grinning.*) It's on! It's on! It's come on!

FRANKIE.
    She's got eyes of lavender, cheeks like a rose,
    A mouth of rosebuds, and everybody knows
    That she's my baby, yeah, my baby, yeah, my baby, oh, oh,
    She's my baby, baby, baby, baby doll.

MARTHA. Me prayer was answered. 'E 'eard me! 'E answered, Archibald. . . .

ARCHIBALD. I switched it on.

MARTHA. I prayed, an' 'e answered.

ARCHIBALD. I switched on. It wan't 'im, it was me.

MARTHA. It was 'im what made yer. It was 'im, Arch, it was 'im.

ARCHIBALD. I switched it on, cos I was sorry for yer.

FRANKIE. (*who continues to sing while they talk*)
    She's got arms that hold you, she's got lips that kiss,
    She's got curves all over, and I tell you, brother, this,
    That she's my baby, yeah, my baby, yeah, my baby, oh, oh,
    She's my baby, baby, baby, baby doll.

MARTHA. 'E made yer, 'E softened yer 'eart. Don't yer unnerstand? It was 'im what softened yer 'eart. Didn't yer feel it? Didn't yer 'eart go soft?

ARCHIBALD. (*doubtful*) Well. . . . it may 'ave done. . . .

MARTHA. An' now, look, 'e's bringin' me my Willie. (*The song has ended, and WILLIE rejoins FRANKIE.*)

WILLIE. Frankie, Frankie, ha, ha. None of your hanky-panky, ha, ha.

MARTHA. My Willie. (*She stands ecstatically before the screen.*)

WILLIE. You sing like a bird, Frankie.

FRANKIE. Thank you, Willie.

WILLIE. Yeah, a cockrel. Ha, ha. (*Shrieks of laughter from the unseen audience, cackle from MARTHA.*)

MARTHA. I love you. 'Ere I am, darlin'.

FRANKIE. Your voice is pretty fowl too, Willie. (*More shrieks*)

MARTHA. That ain't funny. 'E's just bein' rude. I don't like that Frankie. Never did.

WILLIE. If my voice is fowl, yours is positively poultry. (*More shrieks, cackle from MARTHA*)

MARTHA. That's it, you give it 'im Willie. (*ARCHIBALD meanwhile stands thinking in front of the centre skeleton.*)

FRANKIE. If my voice is poultry, when you sing it's positive chickanery. (*More shrieks*)

MARTHA. If 'e talks about my Willie like that again, I'll sock 'im. I will, so 'elp me. Come on, Willie, reply!

WILLIE. It's obvious, from what you've been saying, Frankie, vat you are getting. . . . far. . . . too. . . . cocky. . . . (*The shrieks begin, but he interrupts them. . . .*) and so. . . . you'll have to be taken down a peck or two. (*Redoubled shrieks from unseen audience and MARTHA.*)

MARTHA. 'E got 'im, 'e got 'im. (*WILLIE winks at the audience.*) Ooooooh! 'E winked at me! 'E winked! Archie, 'e winked at me. At me! Oooooooooh! (*She falls in a faint.*)

FRANKIE. Your sense of humour is becoming really eggceptional. (*Shrieks*)

WILLIE. Well, there's nuffing more I like than a good yolk! Ha, ha. (*Shrieks*)

MARTHA. (*getting up*) Oh Willie, 'are you still 'ammerin' 'im? Archie, Willie winked at me. D'you 'ear? Me prayers 'ave bin answered. I could die 'appy at this moment.

WILLIE. What about anuvver song, Frankie?

FRANKIE. All right, Willie. Just for you.

MARTHA. Oh, if 'e's gointer sing, I don't wanter 'ear 'im. I don't know why they 'ave 'im on the programme. An' they should let my Willie sing more—'e's got a lovely voice. (*FRANKIE starts to sing.*) Switch 'im off please, Arch.

ARCHIBALD. Eh?

MARTHA. Switch it off please. (*ARCHIBALD switches off.*) Yer see, 'e answered me prayers. There is somethin' to 'ope for.

ARCHIBALD. But it was me what switched on.

MARTHA. 'E softened yer.

ARCHIBALD. I'd ave to open 'is skull, Martha.

MARTHA. You don't 'ave to. Leave 'im. So long as we know, what's it matter? Leave 'im, leave 'im alone. (*There is a new excitement in both of them, and the contact between them now seems almost pleasant.*)

ARCHIBALD. I was softened. It come inter me sudden, like it was from outside.

MARTHA. It's 'im. An' 'e's sent me my love, too. I tell yer, Archibald, everythin's gointer be all right. We're gointer 'ave 'appy lives. If only I c'd get my Willie 'ere again, wivout that Frankie. If I c'd only 'ave 'im in 'ere again alone. Oh Willie. (*She sees ARCHIBALD is not listening, and her new found love for the world shows in her concern for him.*) And perhaps you can get on the telly again through Willie. 'E might give you a spot every show. Would yer like that?

ARCHIBALD. I wouldn't mind it, Martha.

MARTHA. I'll see what I can do for yer, anyway.

ARCHIBALD. Thanks, Martha.

MARTHA. But we gotter get 'im 'ere. D'yer think. . . . if I was ter pray again it might 'elp?

ARCHIBALD. I dunno. You done it once terday. Don't wanter take liberties, do we? Mustn't overwork 'im.

MARTHA. P'raps if we was ter think of another thought, then we could phone fer Willie again, an' 'e would come.

ARCHIBALD. Another thought. I dunno.

MARTHA. We could try. If yer could just find one, so we could tell Willie ter come. I love 'im so much! Let's think fer a thought. (*They both concentrate hard.*)

ARCHIBALD. What about, when a man wants ter know the truth 'e must seek for it?

MARTHA. (*doubtful*) It ain't very beautiful, is it?

ARCHIBALD. I dunno, depends 'ow yer say it.

MARTHA. It ain't their style. Try fer somethin' like yer last one. That was really beautiful.

ARCHIBALD. Ah, but that sort o' thought only comes once in a lifetime. (*More concentration*)

MARTHA. What about, a woman's work is never fun?

ARCHIBALD. No, that's stupid. It's got ter be clever. (*More concentration*) What about, food fer the belly and telly for the soul.

MARTHA. Eh?

ARCHIBALD. Food fer the belly, an' telly fer the soul.

MARTHA. Don't get it.

ARCHIBALD. Whatcher mean, don't get it, it's plain enough.

MARTHA. I don't see what's clever in that.

ARCHIBALD. It rhymes.

MARTHA. No it don't.

ARCHIBALD. It does. Belly, and telly.

MARTHA. Well yer might as well say, my hand and yours.

ARCHIBALD. Whatcher mean?

MARTHA. It rhymes.

ARCHIBALD. Where?

MARTHA. Hand, and. It's stupid. We got ter do better than that.

ARCHIBALD. Well it ain't much use my suggestin' all these beautiful thoughts if you're just gointer say they're all stupid. That don't get us nowhere. If you don't like my thoughts, then think one up on yer own.

MARTHA. No, keep calm, pet, keep calm. It's fer both our sakes. It's got ter be good. What you said was O.K., but you set a 'igh standard don't forget, an' the public'll spect somethin' really top from yer.

ARCHIBALD. It's true, yer right. We gotter think. (*They think.*) Couldn't we just phone 'im 'an tell 'im we got a thought, like we did last time?

MARTHA. You mean an' not 'ave a thought?

ARCHIBALD. Yes.

MARTHA. I wouldn't like ter deceive 'im, Arch. I wouldn't like ter get 'im 'ere under false pretences. I don't want 'im ter know yet that I'm chasin' 'im. 'E's got ter seem ter be chasin' me. We got to 'ave a thought. An' anyway, if you're gointer be on the telly, you'll 'ave ter 'ave a thought ter say, won't yer?

ARCHIBALD. That's true. Only it ain't so easy.

MARTHA. Think, Archie, get your great brain to work. (*They think.*)

ARCHIBALD. If yer take a short cut, yer might lose the way.

MARTHA. That's what you said yesterday.

ARCHIBALD. Yes, I'm tryin' ter think along those lines. What about, if yer take a day off, yer might lose yer pay?

MARTHA. It's better. It's better, Arch. Only it still ain't Number One.

ARCHIBALD. No, I can feel it meself. It ain't quite up ter that 'igh standard what I've set. (*More thought*)

MARTHA. Somethin' entertainin'. Somethin' witty, like Willie 'isself.

ARCHIBALD. 'Ow about, Willie's silly, but Frankie's cranky?

MARTHA. It's clever, but I don't like to 'ear my Willie called silly, it ain't right. Find another rhyme fer Willie.

ARCHIBALD. Billy, gilly, nilly, chilly, spilly, skilly, rilly, prilly. . . .

MARTHA. Prilly. Willie's prilly. That's it.

ARCHIBALD. But there ain't no such word as prilly.

MARTHA. Then it's original, ain't it? That's what they want. Yer remember 'ow they was upset by the clichy. They wants it ter be new. Willie's prilly, and Frankie's. . . . now then, another word. You say some, an' I'll pick one.

ARCHIBALD. Clanky, swanky, chanky, tranky, flanky, manky. . . .

MARTHA. Manky, that's it. We've got it. Willie's prilly, an' Frankie's manky. Phone 'em up.

ARCHIBALD. I ain't got the number.

MARTHA. Oh, I got it, in my dress. Don't look, Archibald. (*He turns round.*) There, I'll throw it across.

ARCHIBALD. P'raps you should phone.

MARTHA. Should I?

ARCHIBALD. With your sexy voice.

MARTHA. I feel shy.

ARCHIBALD. No, you should phone. Come on, we'll cross over.

MARTHA. D'yer think so?

ARCHIBALD. Come on. (*They change sides as before, crossing themselves as they pass the centre skeleton.*)

MARTHA. (*in a low voice, as she crosses herself*) Help me, Lord. Now then. (*She pulls the phone out, and dials.*) I wonder if it'll be 'im. 'Allo? Willie? (*Now she puts on her 'sexy' voice*) Hellooo Willie dahling—this is four million naine hundred and seventy-six. How are you, my deah? Ai've been watching your delaightful programme again, my deah, you were simply mahvellous—maahvellous. Now listen, Willie, are you listening. . . . Ai hev a thought for you—yes, a brand new thought if you care to come along tonaight, Ai'll tell it to you. Only Willie, Willie, alone, darling. Don't bring Frankie. You understand, don't you? Yes, deah, four mioolion, naine hiundred, and sieventy-sex. You don't remembah me? Nevah mind, you soon will, mai love, you soon will. And I love you too, darling. Good-byeeeee. (*She hangs up.*) 'E's comin'. 'E'll be mine ternight. P'raps 'e'll take me away, Arch, far, far away. (*A sudden thought*) 'Ere, Arch, if 'e takes me away, what'll you do?

ARCHIBALD. I dunno. Would yer leave me, then?

MARTHA. I'd 'ave to. It's me destiny. I'd 'ave ter go.

ARCHIBALD. Then I'd stay 'ere wiv me Mum, an' 'im.

MARTHA. An' me dad, would yer look after me dad?

ARCHIBALD. It would depend if you was comin' back or not.

MARTHA. I wouldn't know, Arch.

ARCHIBALD. If yer didn't come back, I'd 'ave ter throw him away.

MARTHA. P'raps Willie'll let me bring 'im wiv me?

ARCHIBALD. (*quietly*) Martha, Willie ain't gointer take yer no-where. It ain't no use buildin' up these 'opes.

MARTHA. Don't Archie.

ARCHIBALD. What's the good? Yer only deceivin' yerself.

MARTHA. No, I won't listen to yer.

ARCHIBALD. The whole idea's crazy, Martha. It's always bin you an' me. We're the only ones who could ever stick each other.

MARTHA. 'E's comin' though.

ARCHIBALD. An' 'e'll go away. It's always the same. We got nothin'.

MARTHA. (*indicating the centre skeleton*) What about 'im?

ARCHIBALD. Empty, like the others.

MARTHA. I don't believe it; you shut up! Anyway, if I can't 'ave Willie, you can't get on telly.

ARCHIBALD. I know.

MARTHA. What's got into you all of a sudden? Misery all of a sudden. (*The door bell chimes.*) It's 'im. Now brighten up, an' get that thought ready to say it good. (*She marches to the door.*) Are yer ready? (*She flings the door open, and a man comes in wearing a floppy hat, trousers that are much too big for him, and a jacket that is much too small for him.*)

MARTHA. 'Ere, who are you?

JOHNNIE. I'm Johnnie. (*His voice is very serious.*)

MARTHA. But I wanted Willie.

JOHNNIE. Willie's dead. I'm Johnnie, I've taken his place. Now, what did you ring for? I'm a busy man.

MARTHA. But I just spoke to Willie on the phone.

JOHNNIE. Willie's dead. His voice was recorded so that people would have the chance to get used to me gradually — to make the change.

MARTHA. (*in a wail*) But I was gointer go away with 'im.

JOHNNIE. Well, you can't — not unless you kick the bucket yourself. Now, I'm a busy man. You said you had a thought for us.

ARCHIBALD. What's happened to Frankie?

JOHNNIE. Who?

ARCHIBALD. Frankie.

JOHNNIE. They're all dead. What was the thought?

ARCHIBALD. Wait a moment, not so fast! We ain't gointer be rushed inter nothin'. You say Willie an' Frankie are dead. What did they die of? When did they die?

JOHNNIE. They died because their contract was up today.

MARTHA. I don't understand it. Willie winked at me just ten minutes ago.

JOHNNIE. Life's like that. The thought.

MARTHA. The thought don't matter no more.

JOHNNIE. What was it?

MARTHA. (*thoroughly cast down*) Willie's prilly, an' Frankie's manky. It don't matter now.

JOHNNIE. We're broadcasting a requiem to them tonight. We'll sing it. Pleasant viewing. (*He goes. There is a long, profound silence.*)

MARTHA. Just like that. Gone, just like that. I don't believe it. I'm going to switch on. (*She switches on. The screen flickers, then we see the words "normal service will be resumed as soon as possible."*) It's true. It's true!

ARCHIBALD. I knew it would 'appen. I felt it in me bones before. I told yer, didn't I? I told yer.

MARTHA. 'Ow did yer know it Arch? What made yer know it?

ARCHIBALD. I dunno. I just knew it. It come to me. Sudden like.

MARTHA. It's 'im. (*She rushes over to the centre skeleton.*) It's 'im! It's 'im what killed 'em.

ARCHIBALD. Oh Martha, you ain't got no cause fer sayin' that.

MARTHA. It's true. It's 'im. The Government's right. 'E ain't no good. 'E killed my Willie. Just as true love was comin' my way. 'E killed 'im, struck 'im down dead. 'Im! YOU KILLED MY WILLIE! (*She strikes the skeleton, which falls to the ground. With her bare hands she tears it apart, while ARCHIBALD watches, helpless and horrified. She flings the bones all over the room, until at last nothing remains near her but the skull. She takes this in her hands, marches to the door, opens it, and flings it out. Then she shuts the door with a bang, and collapses, breathless, into the armchair.*) Now we can 'ave some peace.

ARCHIBALD. An' we'll never know the truth.

MARTHA. Damn the truth! Damn everything! (*Silence*) I'm very unhappy. (*She starts to cry. Silence broken only by her sobbing, which abates after a while.*)

ARCHIBALD. Didn't like that Johnnie much.

MARTHA. 'E's a sod. Not like my Willie. Willie was so gentle and kind. D'you remember 'ow 'e used to wink at me, an' nod an' smile, like 'e could 'ear my thoughts? D'you remember? You do remember, don't you? Say you remember, Arch!

ARCHIBALD. I remember.

MARTHA. Thanks. (*Silence*)

ARCHIBALD. Martha, we've come to the end.

MARTHA. Whatcher mean?

ARCHIBALD. We've got nothing' left.

MARTHA. Nothin'?

ARCHIBALD. It's all gone. The skulls are empty, yer've destroyed. . . . 'im; an' Frankie an' Willie 'ave left us. What 'ave we got?

MARTHA. We've got nothin'. We've got the phone. Maybe the phone'll ring.

ARCHIBALD. It never rings, you know that.

MARTHA. We've got each other.

ARCHIBALD. Yes, there's that. But 'avin' you's as bad as 'avin' me. We don't 'elp each other.

MARTHA. I know. But it 'elps to 'ave someone there just the same don't it?

ARCHIBALD. I suppose so. I suppose so. (*Silence*) Maybe Johnnie'll be all right when he settles in.

MARTHA. E'll never be a patch on my Willie. No-one c'd ever be like my Willie. Them jokes, an' that lovely smile. Even 'is protrudin' teeth was beautiful. There'll never be another Willie, y' know. Never. I don't think I wanter watch the telly fer a long time. Not fer a long time.

ARCHIBALD. What we gointer do then?

MARTHA. I dunno.

ARCHIBALD. What do other people do?

MARTHA. What other people?

ARCHIBALD. I dunno. Other people?

MARTHA. There ain't none — unless they're up in Mars or somewhere.

ARCHIBALD. (*with increasing despair*) But we can't just sit 'ere, Martha! We can't just sit 'ere. We'll die soon.

MARTHA. An' I'll be with Willie again.

ARCHIBALD. Martha, you don't understand, we're alive now. An' we've got to find somethin' ter do. Martha, what we gointer do?

MARTHA. Me eyes are 'urtin' now.

ARCHIBALD. Martha!

MARTHA. 'Ow, they 'urt. Ow! Ow! Oh, Arch, I've gone blind! I've gone blind!

ARCHIBALD. Martha, what we gointer do? Answer!

MARTHA. I've gone blind, Arch. Where are yer? Say something! Where are yer? (*She has stood up, and gropes around her half of the room.*)

ARCHIBALD. Everythin's gone quiet, ain't it? Funny, me eyes are 'urtin'.

MARTHA. I must keep calm.

ARCHIBALD. I must keep calm.

MARTHA. I've gone blind, that's what's 'appened.

ARCHIBALD. Everythin's dark, so I must 'ave gone blind.

MARTHA. An' I can't ear nothin', so I must 'ave gone deaf.

ARCHIBALD. An' everythin's quiet, so I must 've gone deaf as well.

(*JOHNNIE's face suddenly appears on the screen.*)

JOHNNIE. Hallo, hallo, hallo.

MARTHA. Ah!

ARCHIBALD. Ah!

JOHNNIE. I'm Johnnie, ha, ha, and I'm going to entertain you for the next hundred years, so keep smiling folks. (*Screams from unseen audience*)

ARCHIBALD. Do you know, Martha, for a minute, I thought I'd gone deaf and blind.

MARTHA. So did I.

ARCHIBALD. Funny. I was quite worried.

JOHNNIE. I'm going to start off by paying a tribute to my dear departed friends Frankie and Willie, whom you will all remember so well.

ARCHIBALD. Gave me quite a turn.

MARTHA. I thought I'd 'ad it.

ARCHIBALD. Good thing the telly come on when it did.

JACK. We've received thousands and thousands of telegrams, and I've just chosen a few to sing to you tonight. The Truthseekers sent us this moving tribute to them: (*He sings.*)

　　Willie's prilly, and Frankie's manky, la, la, la, la.

　　Willie's prilly, and Frankie's manky, la, la, la, la.

MARTHA. Our thought! Arch, our thought!

ARCHIBALD. I could 'ave sung it better than that.

MARTHA. All the same, it was ours, on the telly again.

JOHNNIE. And we have had thousands of others, all equally sincere and equally touching. Thank you, friends, on behalf of the dear departed. Thank you. Now we shall have a ten minute silence in their honour. (*A sign flashes on to the screen — "Ten Minutes Silence in honour of Frankie and Willie."*)

JOHNNIE. (*only his voice being heard*) Now get us a bloody script, will you? Get a move on!

ARCHIBALD. D'you feel all right now, Martha?

MARTHA. Yes, I think so. An' you?

ARCHIBALD. Yes. I've 'ad an idea. Somethin' we can do.

MARTHA. What?

ARCHIBALD. Put. . . . 'im. . . . together again.

MARTHA. What, you mean collect up all the bits, an'. . . .

ARCHIBALD. An' put 'im together again. It'll be somethin' to do.

MARTHA. All right, if that's what you want. I'd sooner watch the telly meself.

ARCHIBALD. I'll tell yer what then. You collect up all the bits on your side, an' chuck 'em over ter me — then I'll sort 'em out.

MARTHA. What about the 'ead?

ARCHIBALD. You chucked that outside, didn't yer?

MARTHA. Yes.

ARCHIBALD. Get it for us, will yer?

MARTHA. (*with a note of cunning*) I'll get it for yer, if yer promise ter leave the telly wires alone, an' yer let me watch.

ARCHIBALD. All right, if you pass me all the bits on your side an' you get me the skull — I'll leave the wires alone.

MARTHA. Done! (*She quickly gathers up the bones on her side.*) 'Ow d'yer want 'em?

ARCHIBALD. Chuck 'em all over the place — everywhere. Then it'll take me longer ter put 'em tergether again. (*She does as he asked.*)

ARCHIBALD. Now the skull. (*She goes out, and comes back a moment later, with the skull.*) It ain't broken, is it?

MARTHA. No.

ARCHIBALD. That's lucky. Now just roll it carefully over. (*She obeys.*) Good. Now everythin's gointer be all right again. Life ain't so bad really, is it, Martha?

MARTHA. It's all right. I miss my Willie, though.

ARCHIBALD. Johnnie'll be all right. Once he's settled, 'e'll be all right.

MARTHA. 'E's got a nice nose. Bit like Willie's. An' 'e sings better than what Frankie did. I like 'is clothes, too.

ARCHIBALD. I ain't gointer touch the skull till I got all the other bits in the right order.

MARTHA. 'E might even turn out to be better than the others, yer know. I *was* gettin' a bit tired of 'em. Not so much of Willie, but the other one, 'e was gettin' on my nerves a bit, y'know.

ARCHIBALD. (*who is on his knees, collecting*) An' when I've got all the bits tergether, I'll make yer lose yer temper, and I'll start all over again. (*The screen flickers.*)

MARTHA. 'Ere 'e comes. (*JOHNNIE appears on the screen.*)

JOHNNIE. And now, ladies and gentlemen, I'm going to sing you a medley of the songs Frankie made famous, beginning with—"Baby yeh, yeh, yeh, yeh, yeh". (*He sings.*)

    Yeh, yeh, yeh. Yeh, yeh, yeh.
    Ma baby's gone an' left me,
    Yeh, yeh, yeh. . . .

MARTHA. 'E's definitely better 'n Frankie.

JOHNNIE.
    . . . "I don't know what to do,
    An' I'm feelin' mighty blue. . . ."

ARCHIBALD. An' one day, I'll crack open the skull, an' find out what the truth really is.

JOHNNIE.
    . . . "Yeh, yeh, yeh,
    oh, oh,
    Yeh, yeh, yeh. . . ."

CURTAIN

About the Playwright

DAVID HENRY WILSON was born in London in 1937 and educated at Dulwich College and Pembroke College, Cambridge. He has lived and worked in France, Ghana, West Germany and Switzerland, combining teaching with theatre. He also held academic posts at the universities of Bristol and Konstanz, West Germany, where he founded the student theatre, for whom some of the plays in this volume were specially written. In addition to these plays, he has had productions at such venues as The Theatre Royal Stratford East, The King's Head, The Collegiate Theatre, the Sheffield Crucible, the Leicester Haymarket, The Cheltenham Everyman, The Act Inn, and also in U.S.A., Norway and West Germany. He has had several children's books published in England and abroad, the best known being ELEPHANTS DON'T SIT ON CARS (Piccolo Books).

SAMUELFRENCH.COM

RHAPSODIES
Rosary Hartel O'Neill

A collection of two plays from celebrated New Orleans dramatist
Rosary Hartel O'Neill:

WINGS OF MADNESS
Southern Drama / 1f / Interior

Set in a tacky funeral parlor on a highway outside New Orleans, a
murdered beauty taunts the audience, exposing her bare unshrouded
back, and explaining why she was murdered. Other imaginary characters–her husband and daughter–add an eerie quality to her already
surreal tale.

TURTLE SOUP
Southern Comedy / 1m, 1f / Interior

A young woman fights for her inheritance. Her "dying" uncle mocks
her life, as well as that of her actor husband. A tirade occurs over
Turtle Soup that culminates in its spillage and her Uncle's guffaws
over his prank. He reminds her that it's April first–All Fools Day–and
he is playing a joke on her.

OTHER TITLES AVAILABLE FROM SAMUEL FRENCH

COCKEYED
William Missouri Downs

Comedy / 3m, 1f / Unit Set

Phil, an average nice guy, is madly in love with the beautiful Sophia. The only problem is that she's unaware of his existence. He tries to introduce himself but she looks right through him. When Phil discovers Sophia has a glass eye, he thinks that might be the problem, but soon realizes that she really can't see him. Perhaps he is caught in a philosophical hyperspace or dualistic reality or perhaps beautiful women are just unaware of nice guys. Armed only with a B.A. in philosophy, Phil sets out to prove his existence and win Sophia's heart. This fast moving farce is the winner of the HotCity Theatre's GreenHouse New Play Festival. The St. Louis Post-Dispatch called Cockeyed a clever romantic comedy, Talkin' Broadway called it "hilarious," while Playback Magazine said that it was "fresh and invigorating."

Winner!
of the HotCity Theatre GreenHouse New Play Festival

"Rocking with laughter...hilarious...polished and engaging work draws heavily on the age-old conventions of farce: improbable situations, exaggerated characters, amazing coincidences, absurd misunderstandings, people hiding in closets and barely missing each other as they run in and out of doors...full of comic momentum as Cockeyed hurtles toward its conclusion."
–Talkin' Broadway

OTHER TITLES AVAILABLE FROM SAMUEL FRENCH

OUTRAGE
Itamar Moses

Drama / 8m, 2f / Unit Set

In Ancient Greece, Socrates is accused of corrupting the young with his practice of questioning commonly held beliefs. In Renaissance Italy, a simple miller named Menocchio runs afoul of the Inquisition when he develops his own theory of the cosmos. In Nazi Germany, the playwright Bertolt Brecht is persecuted for work that challenges authority. And in present day New England, a graduate student finds himself in the center of a power struggle over the future of the University. An irreverent epic that spans thousands of years, *Outrage* explores the power of martyrdom, the power of theatre, and how the revolutionary of one era become the tyrant of the next.

Lightning Source UK Ltd.
Milton Keynes UK
UKOW04f0715050913

216586UK00001B/2/P